PRAISE FOR APPALACHIAN MOUNTAIN MYSTERIES

"A real treat, highly recommended for its fine attention to both detail and the psyches of investigators who confront themselves as much as the threat at hand." **~Midwest Book Review**

"GREAT !! BOOK Lynda McDaniel can write. This is one fine read. READ THIS ONE." **~Wooley, Amazon Vine Voice Reviewer**

"The most satisfying mystery I've read in ages." **~Joan Nienhuis, 1% Top Reviewer Goodreads**

"Five Stars! Lynda McDaniel has that wonderfully appealing way of weaving a story, much in the manner of Fannie Flagg. The tale immediately drew me in, into the town, into the intriguing mystery. A real treat to read." **~Deb, Amazon Hall of Fame Top 100 Reviewer**

"Thoroughly enjoyable and intriguing with descriptive powers and beautiful mountain scenery. Intense family and friend dynamics with character vulnerabilities and complex relationships that steal the reader's heart and make this mystery a must-read." **~Pam Franklin, international bestselling author**

FINDING BOOKS YOU LOVE
JUST GOT EASIER

SPELLBOUND MYSTERY MAGAZINE

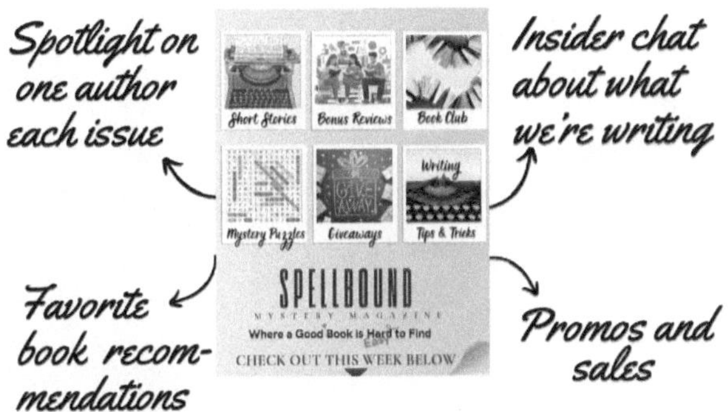

MULTIPLE MYSTERY AUTHORS
IN EACH FREE ISSUE

SUBSCRIBE FOR FREE AT
HTTPS://SPELLBOUNDMYSTERYWRITERS.SUBSTACK.COM/

OR SUBSCRIBE BY CLICKING HERE

Unwrapped

An Appalachian Mountain Christmas Mystery

Lynda McDaniel

Published in 2025 by Lynda McDaniel Books.

ISBN: 979-8-88896-498-9

Printed in the United States of America

Dedicated to my sisters,
both family and found:
Sandy Philp
Angie McDaniel
Virginia McCullough

Inasmuch as ye have done it unto one of the least of
these my brethren, ye have done it unto me. Matthew
25:40

Prologue
Abit

Laurel Falls, N.C.
Autumn 2012

"DELLA," I SAID IN a half-whisper. "I'm reading a book about a girl who may have been killed."

I'd asked Della Kincaid to step into the kitchen so we could talk private. She and her ex-husband/boyfriend, Alex Covington, had joined me and my two boys for supper, the same day as I'd uncovered the girl's story.

"Well, if it's a good mystery, let me read it next."

"No, I mean it's a diary, in the girl's own hand."

Della went quiet. I could tell she was turning over what I'd just said. "What did she write that makes you think she came to harm?"

"She told the saddest stories and then just stopped."

"Teenagers and their diaries—they can start and stop on a whim."

"Mid-sentence?"

"Oh. Maybe you'd better start at the beginning."

Chapter 1
Abit

"Lost: One Chuh-hooa-hooa."

It took us a minute, but then my boy, Conor, and I started laughing our heads off. We had to explain to Vern, my younger boy, that the radio announcer was talking about a Chihuahua dog. You couldn't blame the announcer. Sure, those dogs are as common round here as varmints (and in my opinion, the little ankle-biters *are* varmints), but if you'd never seen that name spelled out, you'd likely pronounce it thataway.

Not long after, though, a wave of shame came over me for making fun like that—especially me, given the way I'd struggled early on at school. That was how I'd gotten my name—Daddy told everyone I was "a bit slow," and well, Abit just stuck. Turned out he was wrong on so many counts, but still, I'd suffered under that curse and shouldn't've made fun of someone else's mistakes. Of course our laughter was miles away and that airwave had already drifted off like a finger of fog in the sun. Besides, you had to laugh at life whenever you could.

Some sadness or other was just lying in wait, fixing to strike.

Our being together on a Saturday morning wasn't all that common anymore. The boys were growing up and enjoyed time with their friends. But this day, we were all home, listening to the local station's Swap Shop program. It was kinda old-timey, but I was glad they hadn't done away with the show. A nice mix of local news, want ads, and for-sale items. I got up to pour more coffee when I heard Conor say, "Daddy, come quick."

Jeb Samson (not the one we'd been laughing at; that was likely his boy) was carrying on about a walnut dresser for sale. Conor had been asking me to make him a dresser for the better part of a year, but like the cobbler's son going barefoot, he was still using an old bookshelf for his clothes. I worked hard to keep food on the table with my furniture-making, and there always seemed to be some project I needed to finish for a paying customer. It had become a sore point between us.

I got back to the living room in time to hear, "Four drawers and in really good condition. The owner said his mama got it when she set up her married home. I'm sad to report he's clearing out the family homeplace after both his parents have passed." Jeb paused a moment outta respect. "Now this fine dresser won't be on the auction block for long. I know you can't see it on the radio, but if you've come to trust me over the years, take my word for it. This is a find."

When I looked round for my phone, Conor was holding his out, already dialed to the number Jeb kept barking at us. Conor had put the phone on speaker so he and Vern could listen to the bidding. I went up against two others, but I was determined to win. When the boys heard the announcer say Abit Bradshaw in Hanging Dog was the proud new owner, they both slapped me on the back and let out a little cheer.

Later, after I'd dropped them off at their school where a soccer game had already started, I headed over to the radio station. Jeb's truck was parked out front. Everybody knew it—the painting on the side said it all: "Samson's Septic. We're #1 in the #2 Business." The Swap Shop job was just a sideline; nearabout everyone round here worked at least two jobs.

Jeb was waiting for me at the door with a big smile. I soon sensed it as part friendly and part con artist. I'd gotten so caught up in the auction that I hadn't considered that "this fine dresser" might not be so fine after all. I looked down where Jeb had set it on the driveway and saw plenty of hours of refinishing ahead. I didn't say anything when I paid up, but I could tell Jeb was mighty pleased with himself—and the cut he'd take.

Didn't matter. Conor was happy, for a change. I planned to set to work on it as soon as I got home. I tried to show both boys how much they meant to me, even if this time it was for Conor. Not that Vern was the kinda boy who needed everything to be tit for tat. He knew he got fair and square. Besides, envy wasn't in his makeup. He'd had a rough upbringing before he came to live with us, and I reckoned he'd never forgotten how much his luck had changed.

I knew it wasn't really the dresser that had Conor acting out. Both the boys were kinda shook up over the fact that their mother and my ex-wife, Fiona, had remarried. Sure, the fellow sounded nice enough, but still, I could tell they were uneasy with yet another change in their young lives. And it'd torn clear through me when I'd overheard Vern saying to Conor how that meant we'd never get back together again. Of course I already knew that, but young'uns' hearts are still open to hope.

I PULLED UP NEXT to my woodworking shop and unloaded the dresser under a maple tree where I liked to work, what with shade in the summer and full sun come winter. The weather had already begun its slide into winter, green leaves leaning into gold and red, some already turning brown. But today carried a warmth broken only by the occasional soft breeze. As I scrubbed off layers of dirt from the dresser, a phoebe told me its name over and over, and a pair of purple martins swooped round the gourds I'd hung for them in nearby trees. They'd be leaving soon for warmer climes, so I took a moment to enjoy their cavorting with the drifting leaves.

I turned back to my work without regret. I liked refinishing almost as much as making something new. The old furniture had a story to tell about the people who'd owned it. Too much polish said one thing. Messages carved in the wood told anothern. Tobacco and wood smoke smothered fine wood, leaving it dried out and neglected, like some folks' lives.

This piece, though, was made from a rich walnut that shone through as I gave it a good cleaning. In the corner of my eye, I could see a squirrel kinda tiptoe my way. Maybe the smell of fresh walnut wood made him think there were nuts nearby. He'd been poking round for a couple year now, though I hadn't seen him lately, stirring worries he'd made his way into someone's Brunswick stew. I'd named him Sparky because of a burned area, hairless and scorched, on his back, likely from some kinda fire, maybe electrical. He sat on his hind legs and chattered at me, not happy to discover I had nothing close at hand for him to eat. "Go over to the birdfeeder, Sparky, and gorge yourself like you usually do," I scolded right back.

"Talking to yourself now, are you?" Matthew said, a big grin on his face.

I had one too when I answered. "Not just *now*. For a long time. It's the only way I can say something without irritating someone, though sometimes I even annoy myself."

Matthew was neighbor and friend, more like brother. Last year he'd moved onto some land I'd sold him, where he built a striking underground house. I'd thought he was growing to love it here following a lifetime in Asheville with all its noise and nonsense, but after a time, oncet his home project was done, he grew restless. He missed teaching, he told me one night as we sat drinking beer by the fire.

I had to hand it to him. This area wasn't known for good jobs, but he'd found himself a teaching position just south of Boone. Not at my old school, The Hickson School of American Studies (aka The Hicks), but some fancy one for rich kids. He was used to dealing with that kinda situation and seemed happy there. But with a thirty-minute commute on good days (way longer during leaf-peeping season), we didn't see enough of each other.

Matthew had been my woodworking assistant while he recovered from an injury, so he spotted the gently figured grain and quality workmanship that became obvious the more I rescued the dresser from neglect. All I could figure was the previous owner had stored it on a porch or in a barn oncet she no longer had a place for it in her house.

"Those are some fine joints," he said, pouring coffee from the electric percolator I'd recently bought for the shop. "And I like your new coffeepot. This is a good addition."

I had to laugh. Back when we'd worked together, we'd both taken plenty of breaks to go to the house for coffee. More to get a little fresh air and some alone time (close quarters in my shop) than to drink more caffeine, which only gave us the jitters. Not smart round power tools.

"In spite of some mistreatment, that dresser looks like something of value," he added.

I took out the top drawer to study the dovetail joints closer. Almost as good as those made by Shiloh, born Bob Greene, who'd worked with me before Matthew. When Matthew left to teach again, I hired a guy named Jason—but I had to let him go last month. He turned the air blue with all his swearing. Thing was, the fellow was as nice and friendly as you please, but when he was working, he'd start cussing and carrying on. At first I thought he'd hurt himself, and I'd drop what I was doing to tend to him. He'd act surprised, like he was wondering what was wrong with *me*. He musta gone into some kinda trance while he worked and became a different person. It was sorta funny at first, such a mild-mannered person acting thataway, but after a while, it wore on me. So it had been just me for a coupla months, which was why I was so behind with my orders.

"Yep, I think this will polish up real smart. Conor should be pleased."

"Is he getting any better?"

Matthew knew about Conor being all angry about his mother, his father, life in general. A teenager. "A little," I said after a lengthy pause. "We're all working through some stuff right now."

He raised his eyebrows, but then looked at his watch. "Sorry, but I need to get a move on."

He was kinda cagey thataway. I think he might've had a date. Some folks did stuff like that on a Saturday night. I sighed, thinking how mine had turned so quiet—unless our bluegrass band, the Rollin' Ramblers, had a gig. Then Annie Totherow came to mind. I'd known her for a long time—all but five year of my life. Her daddy was a beekeeper, and when I was still a boy, I helped Della pick up cases of his famed sourwood honey for Coburn's General Store. I still remember visiting Annie's house and passing by her room, all pink and pretty. Smelling nice too.

I turned back to the dresser and got two more drawers out, but I had to fight with the middle one. It seemed caught on the frame and came out only halfway. I pulled hard, but that dang thing wouldn't budge. I figured the bottom had drooped, though when I looked inside the drawer, the part I could see appeared to be level with the sides. Same thing when I turned it over.

Looking back, I wondered how different life would've been if I'd left that drawer alone. It, or rather what was inside, turned everything upside down.

Chapter 2
Abit

OH BROTHER! I'D LOST all track of time. The boys would be standing alone outside the school if I didn't get over there *now*.

I left the dresser on my workbench and called for Mollie. She often slept in her bed in the woodshop while I was working, but something had made her stir and go searching for goodness knows what. Most of the time it was nothing; just an odd sound or bird caw. One time it was Matthew nearabout dead in the creek, but I doubted anything that serious was going on this day.

Soon enough, she came running, her wiry coat pressed back by the wind, and hopped in through the truck's passenger door I'd opened for her. Not far behind came Red, Matthew's Irish setter. With Matthew gone so much, Red was like our second dog, something that was fine with Mollie. Not so much with me since Mollie spent less time with me now. But I knew that was how it should be, her having fun with her own kind. I motioned for him to run on; we didn't have room in the truck for that big galoot.

All the way home the boys chattered on about this and that. Now that they were getting bigger, Mollie had to squeeze into the footwell, but didn't seem to mind. (I never did hold with putting dogs in the open bed of a pickup.) I was too busy worrying about that ornery drawer to pay much heed to what the boys were saying.

"Daddy, you're not listening."

"I'm sorry, Vern. What did you say?"

"I said Annie Totherow was at the soccer match."

"Yeah, I think one of her sister's kids or grandkids plays ball."

"She wasn't with a kid. She was with a *man*."

His words flew at me, sharp like a slap. Annie again, filling my head with troubled thoughts.

Back home, I got the boys settled in with an afternoon snack and headed for my shop. As I was driving, I'd seen in my mind's eye a little ribbon barely sticking up inside that difficult drawer. I'd missed it earlier that morning, and I kinda chuckled when, sure enough, the thinnest piece of ribbon lay along the inside edge of the drawer. I pulled on it and up came the so-called bottom, revealing a secret compartment. It was less than a coupla inches deep, so the naked eye didn't really notice the drawer was more shallow than the rest. And that ribbon? Probably something a mama or daddy would dismiss as something from a girl's nighty or underwears.

Inside the compartment lay an old book with DIARY stamped on the leather cover, the gold rubbed off long ago, the leather binding chewed by critters. I leafed through it careful-like, not wanting to damage the brittle pages. I found entries on the first thirty or so pages, then nothing.

I needed to finish restoring the dresser (I'd promised Conor I'd get to it right away), but truth be known, I really wanted to sneak off and read that diary. I saw some writing on the first page that said it had been a Christmas gift in 1947 to a Daisy Dawson, age 12 year old.

On the next page, the words held so much promise, my chest ached.

I love you, new diary! Thank you, Cousin Evie, for the perfect Christmas present. I always love the cards and gifts you send. I wish we saw more of you!

Then she added:

I can't wait to write more about all the wonderful things the next year holds.

A cold finger ran up my back. To be honest, I was eat up with superstition, and I'd lived long enough to know there was good reason for that. Soon as you say something is wonderful or perfect or happy, something comes along to spoil it. I'd seen it happen time and again.

I smiled at the loopy handwriting and the innocence of her words. I skimmed through the first ten or so entries, and they were along the same lines. Until.

He is already gone when I get ready for school. Breakfast is cold cereal, but it tastes good by the fire. At school I eat the sandwich Mama packed, swapping halves with my best friend, Amy. Then we spend time in the library, where I check out a book about wildflowers. Mama says she knows more than that book could ever tell me, and I figure she's right. What I can't tell her is it's easier to look in a book than to listen to all her stories about how hard she's had it. I know that's probably true, but get in line! I'm too tired to write more. I didn't sleep well last night. Good night, dolly on the windowsill. Good night, Amy. Good night, dear sister.

I put the book down. I *had* to get back to the dresser, work I couldn't rush. I'd just end up having to redo corners not cleaned right or sand off sloppy coats of finish. By the time I'd finally gotten the dresser fixed up good enough to put on the first coat of linseed oil, the sun had slipped low behind the mountains, swallows sweeping away the remains of the day. I headed to the house to make supper for me and the boys. I took the diary with me.

That evening, oncet we'd all settled down for the night, I got in bed, pulled up the quilt before Mollie hogged it, and looked forward to reading Daisy's diary. But like the page I'd read earlier, the stories took a troubling turn.

Last night no one came into my room, leaving me to sleep in peace. Today is Saturday, and by the time I wake up, everyone is gone. I take Winnifur for a walk in the woods. That's what I call our little feist because her name is Winnie, and she's got such long, beautiful fur. We walk toward my favorite place, near a small waterfall. I'm humming a tune I love—"Will the Circle be Unbroken"—when he steps out from behind a tree. He knew this was the trail we'd take. Once he's finally gone, I wash my face and hands and legs in the cool water.

After reading a few more entries about how scared she was of *him* (as though she didn't dare write *Daddy*) and crying because she was hurting, I felt that ache in my chest come back, snaking its way up my throat and stealing my breath. It felt like this book would strangle me if I read one more word. I set the diary down and cut the light.

I needed sleep, but I kept imagining a little girl writing those words. Maybe she'd had a flashlight under the covers, or if she were really brave, she'd sit upright in bed, declaring with her pen that this was what happened and it weren't right. Something about her strength, imagined or real, soothed me. I finally slept.

THE NEXT DAY, I set the dresser outside again to put on another coat of linseed oil. I looked round for Sparky or Phoebe, but they'd taken shelter against the gusty wind and the falling temperatures. I soon realized I'd need to work inside unless I wanted dust and twigs embedded in the finish. I dreaded the smell of the linseed oil; I already felt a bit off thanks to that diary. Those stories had disturbed my sleep, leaving me unsettled and more than a little queasy.

It reminded me of those times after Fiona left when I could barely come out to the shop. I hadn't felt like doing any woodworking, but I'd needed something to do with my hands. I turned to carving; the familiar, repetitive motion always calmed me. But back then I wasn't of a mind to whittle a pretty little deer or curled sleeping cat. I needed my hands to fashion something of substance. That was when I got the crazy idea to carve a sawed-off shotgun. Just what I needed to draw out the hard feelings wrapped tight round my heart.

I'd rummaged in my scrap pile 'til I found some good-size maple and walnut scraps. I drew up my plans and started to whittle. It took me a few weeks carving, then sanding and finishing 'til it shined. I had to chuckle when I held it. Even to me it looked like the real thing. That had been a coupla year ago, but I still kept it by the front door, just in case.

As I moved the dresser back inside, I sensed something coming up behind me. My nerves raw from that diary and thoughts of shotguns, I grabbed a scrap of rough lumber and turned, ready to strike.

Just a scrawny ol' cat sniffing out something to eat. Other than being too thin, he was a good-looking black cat with a white chest and white socks. While he rubbed round my legs,

I thought about how we hadn't had a barn cat since Peepers disappeared. If you've got a barn, you need one, especially if you have anything valuable stored inside. And I did. But things had gotten so crazy round the time Peepers went missing that I'd forgotten to find anothern. I hated to think what the rats and mice might have gotten up to left on their own.

As I reached down to pet the cat, my phone rang and startled him. He scurried deeper into the barn.

"Have you finished that diary yet?" Della asked the minute I answered. She had that tone she gets—like a foot tapping, impatient. "I'm dying to read it."

I sighed. "No, I can't read much at a time. Last evening, I read a few entries but had to close it."

"That boring?"

"No, just the opposite. That young girl I told you about had a daddy meaner than mine—by a long shot. And later when I turned out the light, those stories gave me dreams from the Devil."

"Oh, now you've made me even more eager to read it."

If I hadn't known Della for almost thirty year, I'd've thought she were a mean person, keen to read the kinda stuff I'd just described. But she'd been a better friend than anyone could hope to have. No telling how I'd've turned out if she hadn't moved next door to my family and taken over Coburn's General Store after Daddy had driven it into the ground.

From what I knew about her past, Della couldn't resist a story like this, good or evil. Back when she'd lived in Washington, D.C., she worked as a reporter and covered a lot of terrible things. So much so her fellow reporters called her "Ghoulfriend." I couldn't figure how she'd turned out so nice, what with all that graft and gore she'd had to write about. But maybe, by comparison, that taught her how precious the good in life was.

"You're just going to have to hold your horses, Della. I found this diary, and I'm gonna read through it first."

"Okay, but hurry up." She hung up without saying goodbye.

Chapter 3
Della

ABIT'S SWAP-SHOP DISCOVERY STIRRED something inside me that had lain fallow for too long. I'd been missing *it*, but until now, I couldn't put my finger on what *it* was. Instead, I'd been wallowing in the doldrums.

I knew some of those feelings came from losing my best friend, Cleva Hall. About six months ago, she went to bed one night and didn't wake up. Surely the best way to go. And she'd had a good life—97 years old. Not long after, two of my favorite customers, Myrtle and Roy Ledford, died within two months of each other. Surprisingly Myrtle went first. Not a surprise that Ross soon followed. Myrtle was so full of life, I'd forgotten she was *old*—91. Or was it 92?

More than one person said I'd been cranky, and I couldn't argue with that. But when I'd heard about the diary, this feeling came over me—a *frisson* I called it back when I still had the fire in me—that I used to get when I'd covered stories as a freelance writer in D.C. I couldn't wait to get my hands on that diary. It sounded like just the ticket to wake up the old me, the reporter who used to find stories other people overlooked (and afterwards sometimes wished *I'd* overlooked).

Abit was busy refinishing the dresser for Conor, so why, I wondered, couldn't I read the diary while he worked? When I pushed him a little, he'd asked what the rush was. Well, he wasn't in the throes of a creative dry spell. I'd been ordering bread and beans, cheese and pickles at Coburn's General Store for twenty-eight years, and though I hated to admit it, I'd grown weary of it.

A couple of years ago, I'd turned much of the store's day-to-day operations over to Annie Totherow. Maybe that had been a mistake. Not in choosing Annie; she was the best sidekick I'd ever had. But in not filling my extra time with more creative ventures. I still did most of the ordering, but I could do that with my eyes closed. Otherwise, I read, did a little gardening, and took my dog, Rascal, on walks in the woods. Not much else to do here in Laurel Falls. That was all nice, but not as the main event. Of course I loved the newfound time with Alex, though he was often over in Chapel Hill for meetings with the magazine he still worked for parttime. And I hadn't had a caper with Abit in a couple of years. The last one—Matthew Ruisseau—felt like forever ago.

I'd have to keep after Abit. I had a strong feeling about that diary.

Chapter 4
Abit

THE NEXT MORNING THE boys and I were eating breakfast when I caught them staring at me. "What?" I asked.

"Something's wrong, Daddy," Vern said in that gentle way of his. "You look, well, funny."

So much for hiding things from my boys. "Oh, just some strange dreams last night. Nothing that bad," I lied, ruffling his shaggy black hair the way Della used to do mine. To change the subject, I asked them if they'd met Cat yet.

"Yeah, when that dog there was chasing it all over the yard," Vern said, pointing at Mollie, who managed to put on her sweetest face. He petted her plume and added, "I think we should rename her. Cat isn't very interesting."

"It's certainly biological," Conor added with a whiff of sarcasm I wasn't used to.

"Well, you boys think on it and let me know a better name this evening. We need to get going."

I dropped them off at school and made my way to Coburn's General Store. When I drove up, I didn't see Della's Jeep. Just as well; she'd've just started bothering me about that diary. Besides, she wasn't the reason for my visit.

When I walked in, Annie musta been in the back. I hung round for a while and was about to leave when she came through to the front. She jumped and dropped a big knife. "Oh, Abit. You startled me. I didn't hear you come in."

"I'm sorry."

"You're sorry way too often," she said, busying herself at the cheese counter. I could feel my face burning. This wasn't going the way I'd hoped. When she looked up, she softened. "Oh, now *I'm* sorry. That didn't come out quite right. I just meant you have nothing to be sorry about. Let's start over. How about a coffee?"

"Sounds good," I said, though I still felt uneasy.

Annie was tall and pretty with long blond hair and a spray of freckles across her nose. She probably had no idea I thought of her as my first girlfriend. I'd sorta hinted at the way I felt on an occasion or two, but she just chuckled, as though I were being funny. We'd stayed friends over time, but nothing more. Well, sure, I was married for more than twelve of those year, but I was thinking more about lately.

When a bunch of customers came in all at oncet, I watched her make interesting small talk with them. I wondered if that was all she was doing with me. Before long, the store felt crowded. Annie looked over at me and made a motion like she was drinking coffee and mouthed, "Sorry."

Me too.

BACK HOME, I CHECKED over the dresser. The finish had a nice, smooth feel after several coats of linseed oil, plenty of dry sanding, and a final wet sanding. I'd fixed the drawer so it closed right and taken out the false bottom. I coulda let Conor enjoy that secret compartment, but I figured he needed to come up with his own way of protecting his thoughts. I carried it to the room he shared with Vern and set it next to his bed.

When the boys got home from school, they went upstairs to change clothes. Pretty soon I heard dresser drawers opening and closing. Not just four times, like the number of drawers, but twelve or sixteen. Conor came downstairs and gave me a big hug, something I'd been missing. Vern did the same and then pulled out some leftovers to help with supper.

Later that evening, I glanced at the diary with dread. I felt I oughta finish reading it, but the latest entries were awful hard to take. Conor saved me from it when he came running in with Mollie, stinking up the place with skunk smell.

"The skunks are back, Daddy. I took Mollie out for a run before bed and one of them nearabout attacked us," he said, trying to catch his breath. "We both screamed—me and the skunk. I'd never heard them make such a sound before—while Mollie barked and barked. I think she scared him as much as he scared me. Its fur stuck out all over like a cartoon character."

He was talking so fast with his hair all mussed up, I almost chuckled. But the stink caught in my throat before I made that mistake. As I pulled out baking soda, hydrogen peroxide, and dish detergent—the best skunk-smell remedy—I promised to get to the bottom of those critters someday soon. Conor and Mollie went off to bathe.

When the boys were in bed, I said good night and was about to turn off their light switch when I remembered the cat. "Either of you come up with any names for Cat?" They shook their heads, and I suggested they give it a few minutes now.

I went to the living room and leafed through a book on woodworking, then put it down and started a mystery set in England. Next thing, I heard the boys quarreling. Mollie raced upstairs to see what all the commotion was about. I followed.

"What's going on in here?" I asked, regretting how much I sounded like my daddy.

"Vern wants to name the cat Ricey Blacky, and I told him that was the stupidest name I'd ever heard."

"It just popped into my head," Vern said, his face flushed.

"It's got a ring to it," I offered, though I had no idea what it meant. White and black?

"Oh, you always take his side," Conor said, looking so grumpy I did chuckle that time.

"Okay, Conor, what do you want to name it?"

He frowned. "I don't know."

"All right. Until you come up with something better, his name stays Cat. It suits him."

"Well of course it does," Conor snapped. "It suits every feline. But it's boring."

Vern rolled so his back was to us, pulling the covers over his head. I turned out their light and closed the door.

"Hey, I can't see!" Conor whined.

"I couldn't agree more."

WHEN I WENT TO bed, I decided to get it over with. Finish that diary oncet and for all. *Maybe the rest of the entries were about nice things*, I thought. And sure enough, the next one talked about a picnic Daisy had with Amy's family, where she felt "a sense of peace." And another on her birthday in April, talking about how fragrant the hyacinths were. Then:

I've started wearing baggy clothes, hoping I'll look so homely no one will bother me. Amy asks what happened to my nice clothes, and I say I've outgrown them. I can tell she doesn't believe me. I've gotten good at reading people's eyes. My plan seems to work for a coupla days. Until it doesn't.

I didn't know much about girls' lives, what with me being an only child and one who didn't go to school for long in Laurel Falls. At The Hicks, most of my classmates were boys, some even grown men. But later watching my boys play, I knew that little Daisy should be making things outta sticks and glue, or playing with dolls. Then again, maybe she'd grown too old for all that, but she could be walking in the woods and pressing wildflowers between pages of the dictionary.

At least her next entry was more along those lines:

I have fun today with Amy. We go down to the creek and take off our shoes and wade. And eat blackberries till our tongues turn black.

I smiled, recalling how me and Cousin Nate used to do the same thing every summer.

That little Winnie. What a faithful companion. I know my Sunday school teacher would say this is unholy, but the way I see it, God is Dog spelled backwards, instead of the other way around.

I nodded, looking over at Mollie, stretched out on the bed as though she owned it. (Fortunately she smelled good after her bath—and had just about dried.) I read on.

He hits me today for no reason. Just sneaks up behind me, twirls me around and slaps me so hard I fall down. Gets up close to my ear, his stinking breath making me gag, and says I'd better keep things between just us, or there is more where that came from. I try to keep my head down, act mute when he's around. He knows it too. When I look up at him, I want to claw the smile outta his eyes.

I knew how long a mean daddy's shadow could stain a life, but I knew nothing about troubles like Daisy was living. I mean they weren't just wicked. They were criminal.

It was hard not to wonder where Jesus was in all this. I knew that question had been asked millions of times, in stories even worse than Daisy's. I remembered the first time I asked it when I was only 9 year old. Mama kinda snorted, "Why would Jesus trouble himself over us? We're just worms in His eyes."

Let me tell you, that sent me into a tailspin. I couldn't make out what she meant. I'd only just come to know Jesus, and best I could tell He loved everyone, even worms. Over time I would reach my own answer to my question, which boiled down to *pray to God, row to shore.* For the most part, our troubles were our own doing, and it was up to us—with guidance from above—to get ourselves outta them. But still, it was hard to understand why young'uns like Daisy were made to struggle so.

Chapter 5
Abit

THAT DARNED DIARY KEPT giving me those shivers I got when something didn't feel right. Everywhere I went, it followed me. In the kitchen, I imagined carrots I was chopping were fingers. In bed, I dreamed awful people were hiding outside my home. In my shop, I pictured saws ripping through ... well, enough of that.

What really made me sad was how, in addition to all the suffering Daisy wrote about, she'd had her childhood stolen. Which she'd never get back. Those thoughts, like green tendrils wrapping round something else nearby, got me thinking about my boys and how fast their childhoods were passing. I was proud they'd grown up so fine, but I couldn't keep away images of them gripping a suitcase on their way to the lives they were meant to live. Like a fool, I tortured myself with such thoughts years before they were fixing to leave, when really I needed to do like Della said: Love them one day at a time.

And maybe they'd stay, I tried convincing myself. But not many young folks round here did; there just weren't enough jobs for them oncet school was over. You had to figure your own way to make ends meet. Find a craft like I did, or run a store like Della. But not everyone could live thataway. Conor would need to travel with his music; he was that good on his fiddle and getting better every day. Vern was showing promise as a cook. Maybe with Asheville getting so fancy, he'd find a place to work when he finished that cooking school he wanted to attend down there.

As if that weren't bad enough, I piled on sad thoughts about Della too. She was getting older, white showing in her oncet-auburn hair. Not *old*—yet—but I'd started trying to grasp the idea that someday my life would need to go on without her, a notion as foreign as telling my boys I didn't love them anymore. And Cleva Hall and Roy Ledford and his wife, Myrtle, (who'd always been extra nice to me, especially back when I could count my friends on one hand after a woodworking accident) had all passed recently, reminding me, and everyone really, that life flowed in one direction.

I stood and shook my head, trying to clear it of such sorrow. What was the point of dwelling on stuff I couldn't change? When the phone rang, I knew it was Della, even before looking. I laughed this time, so happy to hear her voice, healthy and alive.

"I'll finish up today," I told her before she could even say howdy. "Then we've got to find out what happened to that poor girl. I'm pretty sure one or more crimes were committed, but best I can tell nothing was ever done about them."

"Get me the book," Della said, "and we'll see about that."

THAT NIGHT, I FINISHED the diary.

Mean ol' Miss McGaughran makes me stand in the hall today during art class—just because I'd scrunched my nose up when she said we'd be drawing desert flowers. I'd pictured some old droopy things that hadn't gotten enough water. I love art so much I didn't want to waste the precious little time we get with dried-up flowers. Later I look those flowers up and see how wrong I'd been.

That passage stirred all kinds of feelings in me. Teachers needed to *teach*, not punish kids for not understanding before their time. That's why they went to school, for crying out loud. I fumed a while over that before reading on.

I want to run away, but where would I go? And how would I get there? Maybe I could ride my bike to

And just like that, the diary ended mid-sentence.

I leafed through the rest of the book. Not even a drawing or a doodle. Nothing.

A little kid planning how to run away. So scared of or scarred by her overbearing father, her heedless mother, and lousy teachers that she had to escape. I knew how many year she'd end up dealing with that when she should've been growing directly into her rightful self, strong and true.

Of course, that was assuming she'd lived another day.

Chapter 6
Della

"Here. Take it. It's brought nothing but night demons into my bed!"

Abit tossed an old leather-bound book on the counter at Coburn's. When I looked up, I saw how the skin under his eyes looked bruised. He wasn't kidding.

"Wow. This must be some diary," I said, picking up the book more gently than he'd thrown it down. It already looked ready to crumble.

"And you can keep it. I've got new troubles of my own," he added, plopping down in the chair next to the register reserved for old folks who had trouble standing. From the looks of him, he qualified.

"Okay, one thing at a time. The book can wait. What's going on with you," I said as I got us both a coffee and sat back down.

"Oh, the boys came back from Asheville this weekend, and Fiona—you know *Mrs. Babcock*—sent a message by way of them. She wants her mandolin returned by Christmas. 'It will be a nice present to me to have it back in *my* family,' she told them to tell me—and that I was lucky to have had it all this time since the divorce. The mando news was bad enough, but I'm angry she involved the boys in our squabbles. And I don't feel like giving her a *present*."

"Do you have much choice? You sure don't want her showing up and demanding it back. Not in front of the boys." As soon as I'd said that, I wanted to kick myself for being so logical. That's what I meant earlier about needing to get back to my old self. I'd've had choice words for that brash Irish lass.

If possible, Abit's shoulders seemed to droop even lower. "Okay, oncet again you're right. I just felt like blowing off steam." He paused and drank some coffee, making a bitter face I knew wasn't from the medium-roast brew. "I reckoned this day was coming. A few weeks ago I bought plans for a fine-looking mando, and last week I picked out a handsome piece of maple. But I'm having trouble getting started. It's only fifty-four days 'til Christmas, and I'm up to my ears in orders."

"Hey, that's good. If you're rolling in dough, why not order one?"

"I'm a woodworker."

"Isn't that different from an instrument maker?"

He frowned. "I want to try."

I didn't have a good feeling about this project, though what did I know about mandolins? "Good luck with that," I said, hoping I didn't sound snarky. He nodded, so I figured we were good. "Now what about the diary?"

"You'll see for yourself. Daisy Dawson is in a world of hurt, and no young'un should know that kind of sorrow, day in and out. Or I should say night after night."

"That surname doesn't sound familiar. At least not around here."

"Well, neither did Holt, back when we were helping little Astrid," Abit said, tapping his foot either to some bluegrass tune in his head or out of nervousness. More likely the latter.

"Yeah, but this is dated 1947—before so many strangers started moving here."

"Listen to you. *Strangers*." Abit actually smiled for the first time that morning.

"Maybe after twenty-eight years I've graduated from being called that," I said, shooing him out the front door.

THAT NIGHT I READ the entire diary. Alex was still away, so Rascal and I curled up together in bed. I read while he slept and dreamed doggie dreams, paws running in sync with soft whimpers.

Abit was right; it was hard going. But I'd read worse. All those years in D.C. inured me to violence, at least the kind you *read* about. (Seeing it firsthand was a different matter.) Even so, I didn't get to sleep until almost dawn.

The phone woke me at ten o'clock.

"Della, did you read it yet?" Abit on me about that diary the same way I'd been on him. I yawned as loud as I could, and he got the hint. "Oh, did I wake you? Sorry."

He didn't sound all that contrite, but at least he went through the motions. "Yeah. I stayed up late reading, and like you, I had trouble sleeping afterwards."

"We *need* to find out what happened," Abit said with such fervor I flashed back on his teenage years when he was so eager to right wrongs.

"Look, Honey, it's hard to say what the crime was. And it was more than sixty years ago."

"Oh, come on, Della. That poor girl wrote ..."

"Yeah, she wrote some disturbing stuff," I interrupted, "but maybe she was a budding novelist. We don't really know what happened. She might have run away or just quit writing in her diary."

"That's why we need to find out."

"You've got orders to fill, and I've got a store to run."

"Annie's doing that."

I chuckled. He wasn't giving an inch. "We can check the Internet."

"Uh, no *we* about it. You're better at that."

"We also need to check with Sheriff Horne."

"You're definitely better at that. What can I do?"

"Well, you could start by finding out who put the dresser up for sale. Go back to that Jeb Goober or whatever his name is and get some information from him."

"I hate stuff like that. Jeb isn't the friendliest guy round."

"You said you wanted to dig into this, so start digging. Tell Jeb you found something you'd like to give back to the previous owner. Only don't let on what that is, just get the name. Make up a story about wanting to know the dresser's provenance."

Abit laughed. He'd learned that word when we'd watched several TV shows involving some serious sleuthing to identify artwork, and provenance figured prominently in their searches. "I'd hardly think a hillbilly dresser had a provenance other than hard times passed on to hard times," he said, "but you're right. This could lead to something besides trouble."

Chapter 7
Abit

I FIGURED JEB SAMSON would be out on #2 calls, so I worked 'til four o'clock before heading over to his business. I pulled in and parked in a space marked for customers. While I waited, a couple of crows entertained me, walking round like they owned the place. They were checking out something that may or may not have been popcorn when Jeb's big truck rolled into the lot. He acted kinda suspicious when he saw me. I reckoned he thought I was gonna ask for my money back or make trouble some other way. I headed him off.

"Hey, Jeb, my boy likes that dresser real good. It shined up and looks better than new." He smiled, nodded, and waited for more. "But I found something inside one of the drawers, and I wonder if you could tell me how to get in touch with the previous owner."

We lived in a small place, and people tended to trust one another. Not like stories I'd seen on TV set in big cities. He hesitated, then asked what I'd found. "Oh, just a charm from a bracelet," I lied with an ease that worried me for about a second. "I thought it might've been his mama's. Maybe he'd want it back."

I braced myself for him saying he'd give it to the previous owner, but he offered up the name faster than a preacher delivers judgment. Turned out the dresser had belonged to a Hoyt Smith, who worked at the filling station out near the falls. It took me a coupla days to get over there.

When I pulled up, an older man working the pumps nodded at me. He'd likely already seen his seventieth birthday, maybe more. He looked like so many men here, face etched by disappointment and hard work, eyes like flint. I got outta my truck and said to fill 'er up. When I asked if he were Hoyt Smith, he nodded again, only this time frowning.

I introduced myself and told him I had the winning bid on his mama's walnut dresser. Like Jeb, he acted all put out, expecting a problem. I wondered what we'd come to that everything was misfortune just waiting to happen. Then again, I reckoned not all that much good news comes rolling over a filling station air hose, ringing a bell. I cooled him off with the same line I'd used on Jeb. "My boy likes it real good. He'll cherish it."

"I hope so. Mother sure did."

"How'd she come by it?" I asked.

"I remember when she got it—a hand-me-down from that Dawson woman she waited on hand and foot. Mother kept it polished and on display in the living room for the longest time. When Daddy died, she moved to a smaller place and stored it along with other things in my barn. I didn't have room in the house for it, either." He frowned again, making me think it might've carried bad memories for him. Then he added, "Beautiful walnut wood, even if one of the drawers always stuck a little."

I worked to keep a poker face, as Della called it. She always said I didn't have a good one, but this time it seemed to work. "Yeah, I sanded that drawer down a bit, and it glides good as new." I skipped the part about taking out the false bottom and finding the diary.

The bell rang again, and he left to wait on another customer. I thought about how lucky I was the *provenance* didn't wander all round the mountains. According to Hoyt, it went directly from Mrs. Dawson to Mrs. Smith to him. I looked up as Hoyt came walking back toward me. Figuring I needed to ward off him clamming up on me, I quickly asked, "Did you grow up round the Dawson kids?"

"I saw them when I helped Mother with weeding and other jobs a kid could handle. Mother worked for that family for years—cleaning, gardening, odd jobs. But we went to different schools, what with living in different counties. Our home sat just over the Avery County line while they lived in Watauga County, a little north of Blowing Rock."

"How many kids were there?" I worried I was asking too many questions, but he seemed to appreciate the chance to talk.

"Well, there was a girl, Daisy. She had an older brother and a younger sister, but I can't remember their names." He looked lost in thought, then added, "That was a troubled family."

No kidding! I thought but asked, "How so?"

"Oh, something dark loomed in that house. Mother hated spending time inside. But she never objected to whatever Mrs. Dawson asked of her, afraid she'd lose her job. It was a pretty good one, as things went back then. That's why she needed my help. Other kids were getting together to play after school, but *I* had to tend to the high and mighty Dawsons. Mother said I should be grateful, but ..." He stopped when he realized how wound up he was getting over something that happened some sixty year ago. He paused for so long I figured our chat was over. Then outta the blue, "That Daisy, she was always so sad," his tone turning kinder. "Crying sometimes, but Mother just said that was what teenage girls were like. I remember thinking I was glad I was a boy."

"Do you know what was making her thataway?"

"Nah. Like I said, Mother chalked it up to her age. I've had girls of my own, and they did a little of that, just part of growing up, you know? But not near so much as Daisy. She was a sorrowful sight, and then one day she was gone. Mother said not to say anything. In fact, *no one* said anything. It was like everyone knew her daddy had taken her to a looney bin. I've always figured he'd locked her up." He thought a moment before adding what sounded like the end of a well-worn story: "For her own good."

I also figured the sheriff back then didn't want to look too closely at the homelife of a fine, upstanding family. I hated that kind of crap, but I reckoned it happened the world over.

I'd spent way too much time chasing down Hoyt Smith and pulling stories outta him. I needed to get back to work. After paying, I turned to leave, but Hoyt stopped me, standing in my way. "Why'd you come out here, asking all these questions?"

I was ready for him. "Oh, I almost forgot. I found this charm when I was cleaning the dresser and thought it might be your mama's." He looked at it and closed his hand round it, tight. I felt a twinge of regret for my lie about a pretty little charm I'd bought at a junk shop the day before.

When I drove off, I eased my mind with thoughts that something was only as valuable as we believed it was. If Hoyt reckoned his mama really had owned it, he'd treasure it.

But when I glanced in my rearview mirror, I saw him toss it in the trashcan.

Chapter 8
Abit

I DROVE HOME IN a hurry; those orders weren't going to make themselves. Mollie and Red greeted me as though I'd been gone a week, so I rassled with them a while and refilled their water bowl. After that, Red sauntered on home; Mollie'd worn him out. She watched him wend his way toward the creek before following me to the shop.

I finished one order, and instead of tackling anothern, I turned to the fiddlehead maple I'd bought for my new mandolin, as pretty a wood as I'd ever worked. Except I *hadn't* worked it. Even though I knew what needed doing next, I hadn't been able to make the first cut. It's hard to rip into something that beautiful. But the Rollin' Ramblers were booked for some holiday gigs, and I couldn't put it off any longer. I kept imagining Fiona showing up at one of our shows and jerking her mando outta my arms.

I ran my hand over the fine grain. So fine to my touch, like petting a silky-haired dog. The more I stroked it, the more the wood spoke to me, whispering what I needed to do to make the right cuts. I turned on the saw.

And held my breath. (Just as well; my lungs already knew too much sawdust.)

I needed to keep my attention on where I was cutting, so I steeled myself against thoughts of Daisy or Fiona or some fool thing that probably would never happen.

A mando was a lot smaller than the furniture I built, making precision even more important. Each piece had to be perfect. When I shut down the saw, I thanked the wood for showing me the way. I'd done a good job.

Oncet the parts were cut and the tools turned off, I sat a while, appreciating the stillness. How, in its own way, the quiet sounded as sweet as bird song or whispered promises in the night. It was at oncet empty and the essence of everything. Things like that used to confuse me, but I'd grown grateful for such mystery.

I picked up Fiona's mando and held it in my arms for inspiration. Memories of the first time I met her at a music festival in Virginia came flooding back. She'd already favored the fiddle by then, but boy, could she make this old mando sing. I loved it—and her—nearabout on the spot. Funny how those feelings slipped away with time and circumstance. I didn't hate her now, but I had to admit I didn't love her anymore. I wondered if that meant I'd never really loved her.

Nah. I had.

She was such a fine fiddler, some folks were saying the Rollin' Ramblers didn't sound as good without her. That was odd to me. It took Della almost twenty-five year not to be considered an outsider (though she'd never be considered *local* if she lived to be 200). But here they were glorifying Fiona who'd spent little over a decade in the area. I reckoned it was her fiddle playing that made her an honorary local. Still, Ida Lee Jaffrey did a fine job replacing her in the band.

I hated to think about our sound falling off oncet I had to give this mando back. It wasn't just that I couldn't afford an instrument as good. It was more about all the time it'd been cradled in my arms, Fiona's arms, her daddy's arms and filled with all those sweet notes. Anything I could build, assuming I could even do it, wouldn't have that music inside.

I could feel my mood turning sour, what with worrying about losing my mando, having to make a new one, and needing to get to my *paying* jobs. I turned back to the sideboard I'd almost finished. Just when I was struggling with the dang cord on the sander, my phone rang. I cursed the interruption, but managed to get one hand free and answered.

"Hey, Honey. I've got news." Della.

"Good, I hope."

"Not sure yet. I've been checking online sites about Daisy Dawson and getting nowhere. First, it was so long ago. Second, her family apparently didn't live in Avery County, and I couldn't find any relatives by that name living nearby."

Before she could go on, I butted in about *my* detective work. "I discovered the Dawsons lived in Watauga County near Blowing Rock."

"How'd you find that out?" she asked, sounding a little wary. When I told her I'd followed her advice about Jeb Samson, which led me to Hoyt Smith, she said, "Great work, Abit. I'll tell Alex. That should help him go deeper."

"About what?" I snapped. I didn't like being squeezed outta the investigation. *My* investigation.

"He got home earlier today, and I talked him into working on this. I promised a home-cooked meal if he'd look into the Dawsons. And you know him, Mr. Online Whiz. He kept working until he eventually made his way to some genealogy sites. He narrowed it down to the mother and father, but couldn't find anything about Daisy or her siblings."

"That doesn't sound so encouraging."

She paused. She could always see right through me. "Ooh-kay, but that's not what I'm excited about. After a few hours of work, guess what he found?"

"Really? You're asking me to guess something I have no idea about?"

"Hmm, seems somebody got up on the wrong side of the bed. I'll leave you to your pity party

with this little tidbit. The Dawsons are related to
your pal Wallis Harding."

Chapter 9
Della

I WISHED I HADN'T hung up on Abit without saying goodbye, but he was in such a prickly mood. Not like him, though I knew he was dealing with a lot. That mandolin meant the world to him. As he worked on the new one, he probably imagined each cut of the saw going straight across Fiona's throat. No, wait. That was more like what *I* would've been thinking.

I'd been excited about Alex's Wallis Harding discovery, and I'd expected Abit to join me. Wallis was one of a kind; I'd never met anyone quite like him. A short man—not much over five feet—Wallis boasted a mane of tangled white hair and a personality to match. And ironed jeans. I was always struck by that detail, not sure if he pulled out an ironing board or sent them to the laundry. Either way was not the mountain way.

We'd first met Wallis when we were searching for a serial killer who used those dreadful murder ballads to inspire his choice of prey. I say *we*, but Abit and Wallis did most of the work while I dealt with a federal whistleblower story. Alex and I both had helped, and along the way I grew to appreciate Wallis's brashness and freshness, though the feeling wasn't mutual. He didn't seem comfortable around women, especially someone with my personality. And even Abit had never heard him mention anything about the mother of his son, Keaton.

My favorite Wallis trait was how he avoided swearing by making up his own curse words. (I had to admire the guy. I rarely made the effort.) He'd bellow phrases like "CRAPPITY, CRAPPITY, CRUD and SAND IN A SANDWICH. Or STORM AND THUNDER and SON OF A BISCUIT, and they got the point across just as well, if not better, than an expletive.

I wished I could ride along when Abit went out to see him, the natural next step in our investigation, but over the years I'd learned that in situations like this, Abit would find out more if he went alone. Mountain folks worked better together, without someone like me tagging along.

Alex had never met him, but he'd heard a lot about what a character—and skilled researcher—Wallis was. And SAND IN A SANDWICH had entered our personal lexicon. I'd need to finagle a way to introduce them.

Chapter 10
Abit

ALMOST ANY EXCUSE WOULD'VE worked to get me outta my shop, but the chance to see Wallis Harding tugged harder than most. I regretted that we'd only seen each other a time or two since we'd worked together to find that killer.

But first I needed to call Della to tell her about Hoyt Smith's notion that Daisy went to a "loony bin." I'd forgotten all about that when we'd talked the day before, what with my sorry mood and all.

She thought the asylum stuff was interesting and said she and Alex would check into it. When I told her I was headed to Wallis's, she sounded happy. She never was one to hold a grudge.

Wallis refused to get a telephone, so I hoped I wasn't wasting time I didn't have to lose. After a windy, thirty-minute drive, I was relieved to see his truck in his drive. I parked so I didn't block him in. He was the type to up and leave in a hurry if he didn't like the way the conversation was going—even at his own house. I knocked on his front door.

"Well, if it isn't young Abit," he said, opening the door just a crack. "What brings you round?"

"Hey, Wallis. I'm looking into someone you're related to." With him there was no point in beating round the bush.

"Coming after my family again?" he asked, giving me a beady-eyed look.

My back stiffened. I knew exactly what he was referring to. When we were working that case, I'd actually gotten the notion one of his kin may have been the killer. Of course I never mentioned my suspicions to Wallis, but he was a sharp one. Not much got past him.

I was still struggling to find a good answer when Wallis reached round the door and punched me in the arm. He chuckled. "I was just funning you, young Abit." I wasn't so sure. People round here carried a grudge longer than coal mines ruint the countryside.

And he hadn't invited me in yet, standing with the door like a shield as I rocked from foot to foot outta nerves. "I'm hoping you can help me find what happened to Daisy Dawson."

"Well, that's a blast from the past," he said, rubbing his stubbly chin. "Haven't a clue. Her mama was from my mama's side of the family. Strange woman. As I recall, they up and left the area, at least some of them did. The others died off. That's as far as my recollections go."

"Come on, Wallis. You know how much you helped us find that killer. I couldn't have done it without you. Your research skills are way better than ..."

"Stop. Stop. I'm welling up." He made a gesture like he was brushing away a fake tear. Then he opened the door wider. "Well, don't just stand there on the porch, letting all the cold air in. Come in, and I'll make us some coffee."

Wallis put a pot of water on the stove and fiddled with a bag of coffee. I lost count of how many scoops he'd put in, and I feared he had too. I remembered how strong he made it, and that I needed to let the last few sips go if I didn't want to swallow a bunch of grounds.

While he waited for the pot to boil, he didn't say much, rubbing his chin and looking lost in thought. I hoped he was trolling through that impressive brain of his for family stories.

"Yes, I remember the Dawsons," he said, pouring two mugs of coffee. "The father wasn't reared here, but his people were from this area. Pretty well to do compared to us. Doctor. Professionals always lived a better life here, though I wonder how many times they were paid in chickens and jars of jam. As I recall, they lived a little north of Blowing Rock in Watauga County."

"What can you tell me about them?"

"Well first, don't you think it would be polite to tell me why you're so blamed interested?" I felt his beady eyes on me again. He motioned for us to settle in the living room.

I sat on the couch and told him about the diary, but I stayed clear of the dark details. Sure, her father wasn't from Wallis's family, so I didn't think he'd get all that defensive, but I needed to be careful.

"So some little girl's diary has you all wound up? What's got into you, young Abit? Next thing I know you'll come around recommending a good romance novel."

I couldn't help but laugh, and that started him cackling. I sighed with relief. I knew he was going to say yes to helping me, and his research could really get this investigation rolling. I reckoned my troubles were over.

Didn't know it then, but they were just beginning.

Chapter 11
Abit

I WAITED A WEEK, hoping each day I'd hear from Wallis. When he finally got in touch, it wasn't quite what I was expecting. I'd gone out to the porch to bring in more wood when my phone rang.

"Uh, young Abit? It's Wallis. Wallis Harding."

As if anyone else called me *young Abit*, especially now that I was well into my forties. "Hi there, Wallis. Whatcha found out?"

"Oh, I found out plenty, but not as you might expect. I'm, er, in jail. Even though *I'm* the one with a broken arm!"

"In jail? Where? And how did you break your arm?"

"I'm in the Newland jail, and that MOTHER TRUCKER sheriff says he knows you. I told him I wish I didn't—you're the reason I'm in here—but then again I don't have anyone else to get me out. You owe me."

"Whoa, wait a minute. How did this all land on me? And what about your son?" I closed the door behind me and dumped the wood in the copper kettle sitting near the wood heater.

"Keaton's off living in Raleigh, and the rest of the family is mad at me. Because of *you*."

I took a deep breath and tried to make sense of it all. I actually looked at the kitchen clock to see what time it was, wondering if maybe I were dreaming—but it read two o'clock. In the afternoon. I knew I'd never get a good answer over the telephone. "Wallis, do you want me to come get you?"

"Something like that."

"Can't talk? Someone listening to you, like Sheriff Horne?"

"Something like that."

"Do I need to bring money?"

"Something like that."

I hung up and called Della. She and Airhorn (Sheriff Horne's loud, harsh voice had earned him that nickname) had a kinda friendship based on professional respect after working together on some cases.

"Hey, Abit. What's up?"

"I'm not sure, but I need your help."

"Anytime."

That was the thing about Della. She never asked questions. No, wait. She asked tons of questions when we were working together on a caper, but not when I needed her. I filled her in on Wallis, as much as I knew, and how we might need her to smooth things over with Airhorn. She said to swing by Coburn's and she'd drive.

WHEN WE PULLED UP at the sheriff's office, we were surprised to find Wallis sitting on the bench out front—his arm in a sling. Della spoke kindly to him and headed inside to deal with the sheriff.

"Good grief, what in the world did you get yourself into?" I asked.

"You mean what did *you* get me into! A family fight, that's what."

"Now cut that crazy thinking out, Wallis," I said, raising my voice to him. "I didn't cause this, whatever *this* is."

I'd never spoken to him like that before, but he was out of his mind. I expected him to bark back like usual, but he just hung his head and kinda whispered, "We can talk on the way home. Please take me there."

He musta had the stuffing knocked outta him. "Are you free to go?" I asked.

"He is now," Della said, marching toward her Jeep. "But not without owing me $125."

"I've got it at the house," he said, not able to look her way.

We drove in silence, me giving Della directions how to get there. Wallis was in the back, where his short stature made his legs stick out from the seat like a little kid rescued from a schoolyard fight. I was dying to ask him what'd happened, but held off.

Della pulled into his drive and cut the engine. "You're home, Wallis."

"Thanks for the ride," was all he said as he opened the back door.

"Not so fast, Mister. This isn't a mercy wagon. We're owed a story." You had to admire her for not mentioning the money.

"I'll put on the coffee," he said, waving his good arm to say *come on in*.

While the coffee brewed, we sat all bunched up on his couch, looking like the Culhanes on that old TV show "Hee-Haw." When Wallis got up to get the coffee, I could tell he needed help, what with his arm in a sling. Oncet we settled back down, I said, "Okay, Wallis, truth time."

"Well, it all started with you asking about the Dawsons."

"Not a good start, Wallis," Della chimed in. "*This* (she smirked as she waved her hand toward his sling) is *not* Abit's fault. Get on with it."

"Yes ma'am."

I knew the *ma'am* would make her madder than him blaming me for everything. I didn't want to get bogged down with them going at one another, so I tried to move things along. "Let's start with who broke your arm, Wallis."

"Okay, truth be known it's not broken," he said, rubbing it pitiful-like, "but it's badly sprained." I rolled my eyes, and I think I saw steam coming outta Della's ears. "I went to see my cousin up in Blowing Rock. Not the brother of Daisy; he's long gone, best we can tell. This one came from a different mother, which I reckon made him my third cousin. Anyways, I started asking about what happened to Daisy, and real sudden-like he got all up in my face, telling me to mind my own business and not talk bad about his family. Firstly, I pointed out to that CRUD MUFFIN that I hadn't said anything bad about *our* family, and secondly, well, one thing led to another, a tussle ensued, and you know the rest."

"Did you get anything out of him, Wallis?" Della asked.

"Not much. Just like you said, little Daisy disappeared one day and no one knew where she went. He remembered how our family fussed over it for a while, but like me, he reckoned her daddy had enough political pull to keep things quiet. So I don't think she was killed. They wouldn't've and couldn't've stood in the way of that kind of investigation." He paused and looked tore up when he added, "I just don't know."

I told him about Hoyt Smith's theory of an insane asylum, but he didn't hold with that. "HORSE FEATHERS! That young'un, from what I could tell, was sharp as a tack. She weren't crazy. It all boiled down to her having a mean father or mother or both. That's the way I see it. You might be surprised to learn this, but my family is kinda strange."

I had to pinch myself to keep from laughing. Wallis was eat up with strange and his son gave Norman Bates a run for his money. Then again, we're all strange in our own ways, even Della.

I held back from asking anything based on what Daisy had written in her diary. We had to keep that to ourselves for now. When Della opened her mouth, I prayed she wouldn't mention it either.

"Could you at least write down your family tree, Wallis, and where they are now, to the best of your knowledge?" Della asked. "We can take it from there."

Wallis nodded and kinda wobbled as he stood. I jumped up to help, but he waved me off. He rummaged round on his desk—still just a card table in the corner of the living room—and after a while came away with paper and pencil plus a wad of bills he handed to Della. He wrote for some time before he spoke.

"Listen, I've caused you some trouble, and I appreciate you picking me up and getting me outta Airhorn's grasp. I'd like to help. I do remember that family would come to reunions my mother mercilessly staged every year, and we all felt like poor country cousins next to them, which we were. Emmet, the daddy, was a prominent doctor, which you already know, but I don't think anyone's mentioned that he died fairly young—heart attack was what we were all told." Wallis put a hand to his chest, likely recalling his own heart troubles when we'd worked together before. "The mother, my aunt, was real high strung and a few years after Daisy disappeared, she fell off a cliff around Blowing Rock. Not *the* Blowing Rock, but nearby. Rumor had it she took her own life, though the official word was accident.

"Don't know much about their kids. The younger ones were about the same age as me, but they didn't want to play with us. Too rough, I guess, for their refined ways. I remember now that Daisy had a baby sister named Violet and an older brother they called Dill. Their mother—*Iris*, no less—sure was into botanical names."

"Do you remember Daisy's best friend, Amy? She mentioned her a lot in the diary." Della and I really wanted to have a good talk with her, and I hoped Wallis could help.

"I do remember her. She came with Daisy to those dang reunions, but I don't know what happened to her. Like I said, we didn't hang out together or anything."

"And Emmet, Daisy's father, was from around here?" Della asked.

"His *people* were from here, but he grew up in Richmond and went to medical school there," Wallis said. "Then he came down here to practice. I always reckoned he wanted to help his people out, but maybe he needed to get away from something."

When Wallis's voice began to fade, I could tell even the strong coffee wasn't enough to keep him awake much longer. He was practically whispering by the time he promised to keep digging. His eyelids were just about shut when we slipped out the front door.

Chapter 12
Abit

"WHAT A CHARACTER," DELLA said when she'd finally pulled offa Wallis's teeth-rattling dirt road and onto the tarmac. "Too bad the diary had already told us most of that information."

"True enough, but we didn't know how Daisy's parents died. Her mother killing herself makes me think she felt bad about something, like not listening to Daisy."

"Hard to say. Maybe she missed her daughter too much. Or maybe she really slipped and fell." Della tossed the money Wallis had given her on the console between us. "Count those bills, Abit, and make sure Wallis didn't cheat me."

I counted ten twenties. "He didn't, Della. In fact, he gave you $200."

"Oh. Well, okay. Nice of him. We earned it. Take a couple of twenties for yourself."

"Oh, I couldn't."

"Why not? You gave up your afternoon for him. Took you away from your work. Go on." She had a point there. Then she added, "Do something special with it—for someone else if you can't accept it for yourself. I'm putting forty dollars in the gallon jar we've got next to the register for little Buddy Ledbetter. He's only 4 years old and needs an operation his family is struggling to pay for because they couldn't afford health insurance."

WHEN I GOT HOME, the boys were already back from school and making themselves a snack. They were growing tall and eating like they were trying to beat Old Man Clendenin at the pie-eating contest.

They'd taken the school bus home, something they hated, but it helped me out on busy days like this one. I looked forward to when Conor could drive. Man, that would be such a help. I had a surprise for him when he turned 16 in a coupla weeks, but for now, I tried acting like I barely knew his birthday was coming.

"I've got twenty dollars for each of you," I said, holding up the two bills from Della. They put down some kinda peanut butter concoction and jumped up to grab them. I held them higher than they could reach (though that wouldn't be for much longer). "Della gave me these by way of Wallis Harding. Remember him?" Vern nodded hard—Wallis, you could say, helped him come live with us—and Conor smiled, likely remembering how they'd met after all that mess settled down. "But she put some strings on these bills. You each have to do something special with yours."

"I need new fiddle strings," Conor said.

"I think we can cover that. Do something out of the ordinary."

They both thought while they went back to their snack. Pretty soon Vern said, "Oh, I know. Danny Ledbetter's brother, Buddy, needs an operation."

I mentioned that Della had a jar for donations at Colburn's. "We'll go down there Saturday."

Conor didn't say anything for a while. I reckoned he was wrestling with doing something for himself or somebody else. He looked kinda embarrassed when he finally spoke. "There's a girl in our class. She's really nice and all, but she never has the money for school field trips. I'd like her to go to the Asheville Art Museum with the class next week." I figured he didn't want us to know how much he'd like to sit next to her on the bus down there and back. "I don't know how to give it to her, though."

"We'll work together on a letter to the principal and I'll sign it. You can deliver it to her office tomorrow."

I was about to give them each a bill when I remembered Cat. "Oh, and you have to rename Cat." I waited and noticed Vern looking uneasy. "What?"

"I tried. It's up to Conor."

Conor made one of his faces again. I gave them the bills anyway.

Chapter 13
Della

I DREADED RESEARCH THAT dated back as far as Daisy's young life because it usually meant enduring the nauseating sounds, smells, and motion of microfiche whirring before my eyes. But this time we'd lucked out. The *Watauga Democrat* had digitized decades-old newspapers, and they said several libraries had access to them.

I could have gone to Newland, but I decided I needed a getaway, even if only to Boone. Alex wasn't interested in a library trip, but I knew who would be.

"Road trip?" I asked Abit as soon as he answered.

"Yes."

Not *where* or *when* or *why*. Just *yes*. My kind of guy. After I filled him in, we set a date for the following Tuesday.

In the meantime, Alex and I checked out regional sanitariums active in 1948, the year Daisy disappeared. Back then, Western North Carolina had earned a reputation as a healing resort thanks to its fresh air, clear waters, and beautiful vistas that seemed to yield lower case numbers of tuberculosis and other respiratory diseases. I'd known F. Scott Fitzgerald had spent a couple of years at the Grove Park Inn during the 1930s, but I'd always thought his stay was about revitalizing his creativity and being near his wife, Zelda, who was committed in the now infamous psychiatric asylum, Highland Hospital. Turned out he was also recovering from tuberculosis, drinking like a fish, and experiencing a tragic mental decline. The so-called "darlings of the Jazz Age" had lost their luster—and their way. Fitzgerald eventually pulled himself together and left Asheville and Zelda for Hollywood, hoping to find fame again writing for the silver screen.

Zelda didn't fare as well. In 1948 nine women—including Zelda—died in a disastrous fire, likely due to locked doors. Laws changed after that, but too late for her, and, I feared, for Daisy. I held my breath as I searched for the names of the other eight women. I had to study several sites before I found a reporter who cared about them as much as a Jazz Age celebrity. I sighed with relief when his list *didn't* include a Dawson.

But that was the sanitarium that had made the news. We found it far more challenging to comb through the other asylums to determine if one had committed Daisy, assuming Hoyt Smith's supposition were even true. Fortunately Alex had some medical connections through his magazine work and spent the better part of a day on the telephone with every hospital open in 1948 and still operating today. His temperament was better suited to that kind of work. I'd've slammed the phone down—or rather, stabbed at the red button on my cellphone—after the third or fourth functionary.

His patience paid off. While he couldn't get anyone to say Daisy had been in their hospital, he got them to confirm she *had not* been a patient. Seemed like splitting ethical hairs, but it worked.

COME TUESDAY, I WAS happy to climb out of the rabbit hole of the Internet. We'd lost ourselves there, discovering all kinds of useless (at least to us) information—tractor accessories for performing surgery on a cow, finger chopsticks, London bus potato art—before turning off our computers Monday evening and enjoying Alex's chicken pot pie with a fruity Orvieto. The lemon custard pie I'd brought from the store wasn't bad either.

On the way to the library in Boone, Abit and I rode along in good cheer. The day had turned sunny once the morning mist burned off, and the trees lining our route entertained with their flamboyant seasonal display. It felt like old times.

Until Abit mentioned Daisy.

"I can't stop thinking about that poor girl. Her words have curled up in my brain, worse than an earworm. I keep wondering why she didn't tell her mother about what her father was doing to her. As sorry as I was as a kid, I'd've screamed for help."

"Easy to say, Honey, but there could be lots of reasons. One, she was a teenager and relatively powerless. And scared. Who knows? Maybe she *did* cry out, but her mother didn't want to believe her. That happens more than you'd think."

"Man, I thought I had a bad father. Hers was the worst."

"We don't know Dr. Dawson was the culprit. Uncles, neighbors, cousins ... they do things like this too."

Abit smirked, and I could tell his mind was closed on the subject. In fact, he'd gone so quiet that after a while I looked over to check whether he'd fallen asleep. I was surprised to see he was wide awake with big, fat tears snaking down his face. I found a wide spot off the road and pulled over.

He held the diary close to his chest, and what I finally got out of him was a deep sorrow—for Daisy and for vulnerable children everywhere. He wiped his eyes and blew his nose. "She was afraid of her Daddy, maybe worse, knowing all the things he was capable of. All of us reared by fathers and mothers who can't care proper-like for their young'uns know that fear, on one level or anothern. Way too many when you start counting. And then we grow up and start spreading our own hate and fear to another generation. Or slip away from life, too damaged to deal with what it threw our way. Some of us, the lucky ones, were born with enough spirit to move forward best we could, especially when someone nice moved in next door."

Well, that did it. We both blubbered for a while. The road trip I'd looked forward to had turned melancholy and grew worse when we failed to find much news about Daisy in the *Watauga Democrat*. Just short society articles about her going off to visit relatives for spring break. They wrote that kind of claptrap back then; maybe they still do in some places. (Thank heavens I never had to.) One was dated 1946, another 1947. In 1948, the year she disappeared, not a word about her going anywhere.

When we got back to the Jeep, I circled around town looking for a diner I thought Abit would enjoy. So many of them closed right after midday dinner that I was about to give up when I drove past the Dan'l Boone Inn. We'd eaten there years ago, but it was a bit pricey for us. Didn't matter this time. The fried chicken, green beans, buttermilk biscuits, and strawberry shortcake were worth every penny. I knew Abit was feeling better when I saw him tuck into his meal. The coffee was good and strong and did its part to get us home safely.

Chapter 14
Abit

I sounded like Jason, shouting swearwords I was glad nobody was round to hear. I'd been working on my new mando and burned myself on the pipe I'd heated to bend the wood for the sides. That was how you got the beautiful shape that sits in your arms so easy. The way things were going, I reckoned this one would feel more like holding a mailbox than a sleeping baby.

I made a pot of tea and sat a while, trying to take my mind offa the mando. So naturally I started thinking on where we stood with our Daisy Dawson investigation. The road trip to Boone with Della had been fun, but as it turned out, not much help. And we hadn't heard a peep from Wallis. I went over in my mind what we did know and got so frustrated I went back to work.

My phone rang and pulled me away from the mando. I was ashamed how easy that was to do. Like if Cat meowed, I'd drop everything to see how he was doing. Anyways, when I answered,

Della told me she and Alex were working on the kinfolk list Wallis had given her.

"We haven't turned up much on Wallis's side of the family," she said, "and Alex is trying to work the father's side but keeps bumping up against the fact that people who'd known Daisy as a child were getting pretty long in the tooth." I was muttering some thanks for their efforts when she interrupted. "But the main reason I called is Alex wants to meet Wallis."

"Oh," was all I could say. I couldn't imagine how that would ever work out. If all three of us descended on him, Wallis would likely feel cornered in his own home, and he'd be stiff as a board at Della's. I explained all that and as we talked, I remembered he favored Adam's Rib, a pretty decent local restaurant. Oncet we'd agreed on that, I told her I'd drive out to his cabin the next day to set things up.

I went back to my mando and carefully touched the sides. They felt cool enough to piece to the front. Oncet done, I wanted to make sure I got the right feel, so I held Fiona's mando and then held my new one. I repeated that a time or two. I could tell I wasn't there yet, though I'd set the bar pretty high.

When I'd first spotted that mando in Fiona's hands, I knew it was special with its beautiful single-piece back. It had the classic F-5 punch, but a particular sweet, songbird quality eager to sing. I believed it was Bill Monroe who advised someone, "You keep that mandolin and play it every day, and it'll become a part of you." He was right. Ever since Fiona'd given it to me, it had been my daily companion, slowly revealing its secrets and occasionally unlocking the ancient tones that connected me to Mr. Monroe's music.

As the years passed, that beautiful instrument just kept opening up and sounding even better. It challenged me to let it realize its full potential as well as my own. I didn't reckon I'd ever pull all those notes I kept chasing and hearing in my mind, but whatever happened, the joy of holding it close and sharing music together was satisfaction enough. I was going to miss it something fierce.

When I looked up from my reverie it was already dark outside, which caught me by surprise. This late in the year the sun set way too early. I needed to heat up some supper for me and the boys before we all headed out to a Rollin' Ramblers' concert in Banner Elk. Not too far away, but I'd need to hurry.

Chapter 15
Abit

By the time I made it over to Wallis's, I'd worked myself up with all kinds of distressing notions. Like he wasn't getting in touch because he'd gotten into another fight. Or had another heart attack. Troubling thoughts like that got me pressing my foot down too hard on the accelerator until one of the switchbacks on his windy road nearabout sent me into a ditch. After that I slowed my truck—and my mind—and finally pulled into his drive.

Wallis's truck didn't ease my fears, but seeing him in the window, reading in his easy chair, did. He stood, and we both got to his front door about the same time.

"Well, I wondered when you were going to check in," he said. I noticed his sling tossed aside on the couch.

"And I wondered when you might swing by or, bold of me to say, *call* me with some news."

"Don't have a GOLDAD phone."

"Like I don't know that all too well. But I assume you go to town from time to time, where they still have payphones. Or when you were out talking to relatives, like you'd promised."

"I'm done with talking to those SONS OF A BISCUIT." He rubbed his arm real pitiful-like. "They don't have good sense." Just when I was about to give up on any news, he went on. "I did talk to one cousin, Ward Calhoun. Lived here then and remembers Daisy, though now he's as old as the hills. It would be wise to quickly follow up on him and any names he might provide."

I thought of the work Alex was doing on the Dawson family and reckoned it was a good time to mention Della's get-together idea. I'd also figured a likely way to get Wallis to respond the way we wanted. "There's a guy—Alex Covington—who's as good a researcher as you. He's Della Kincaid's ex-husband/boyfriend."

"WHAT IN THE SAM HILL does that mean?"

"That he's researching the Emmet Dawson side of the family."

"No, about the ex-husband/boyfriend. Is that one person or two?"

I started laughing, following his logic. "It's one, and a long story." His beady eyes studied me a while, but I held out. I knew what really bothered him was me saying Alex was as good a researcher as he was.

"And why does he want to meet me?"

"To compare research notes. I bet you've got way more than he does." Just egging him on.

"I might. Hmmm ... where would we meet?"

"They want to buy you dinner at Adam's Rib. Next Tuesday if you're available."

"Who knows what'll happen by next Tuesday? How about today?"

I pulled out my phone. "These are handy things, Wallis. You might consider ..." He waved me off, motioning me back to the phone. When Della answered, I said, "Wallis wants to go to Adam's Rib today. Uh-huh ... Okay ... Will do."

"I'm starving," Wallis said when I put the phone in my pocket.

"We're about to fix that."

ON THE WAY TO The Rib, as locals called it, Wallis said he needed to use my phone. I decided not to rub it in again about him needing his own. While I drove, he poked and prodded the keypad like he knew what he was doing.

We got to the café before Della and Alex so I coaxed Wallis into a chair across from where I'd make sure Alex sat. I knew Wallis wasn't crazy about Della, but if I were her, I wouldn't take it personal-like. He's not exactly the kinda guy who cottons to women's ideas. I could tell by the way he looked at his shoes when she talked to him. Or how he'd take the conversation in a different direction without even a nod to what she'd just said.

To my surprise, Wallis stood like a gentleman when they came in. As he shook Alex's hand, he said, "Pleased to meet you, sir. I looked you up online just now. Impressive body of work."

I nearly fell offa my chair. I'd never heard him compliment anyone other than Keaton or himself. And oncet in a while me, back in the day.

"And I've heard nothing but amazing stories about you. Fine work on that serial killer a few years back."

"More than a few. I've lost most of my hair since then." He lifted his leather hat a bit and let it fall back in place.

"Well, given that investigation, I'm surprised you didn't lose it all *then*."

Wallis was eating up the attention, but I could see Della getting fidgety with all the brotherly love. Before she could say something to break the harmony, I said, "So let's put all those investigative skills to work to find justice for Daisy."

From the look on Wallis's face, I reckoned I'd blown the mood worse than Della would've. "We're getting there, young Abit. We were headed thataway, but you just put SAND IN A SANDWICH."

Della and Alex looked at each other. Della couldn't hide a smile.

"What? You making fun of me?" Wallis asked, frowning. Pretty soon, though, I saw his lips curl into a smile of his own.

We finally got down to work. First thing: ordering. This time I got the special: roast chicken with sweet potatoes and green beans. Wallis and Alex ordered steaks, sealing their newfound bond. Della surprised me and ordered the same as me. Like we were on competing teams.

Wallis answered a lot of Alex's questions while he was chewing, spewing bits of food here and yonder. I was glad I was on the same side of the table as him.

"It stands to reason, if that word can be used in the same sentence with my family, that I know more about *my* relatives, including one distant cousin who's in his nineties, but they say he's still pretty sharp. I can't get too involved, you understand, because it's been a family secret so long, it'd be like I'd dug up a grave and robbed it. But you, Alex, could go see him. He still lives just south of Blowing Rock."

I heard Della let out an indignant *harrumph*. I nudged her under the table, and she managed not to start any trouble. I felt kinda bad—she'd always stuck up for me—but the way I saw it, we needed to get as much outta Wallis as possible, and then we could go off on our own.

"So these are cousins on your side of the family, that is, Daisy's mother's side. What about the father's side?" Alex asked. He was doing that reporterly thing of asking what he already knew. And it paid off.

"That would be Burt Seely. He can fill you in better than I can. To be honest, things get tangled up enough that some of them are cousins on *both* sides."

Alex cut into his steak, then put his knife down. "Those are good sources to follow up on, but I have a feeling you know something else, something we don't have to go pull out of strangers."

Wallis chuckled. "You SON OF A BISCUIT. Got me there."

I had to hand it to Alex for breaking through that hard shell, but Della was rolling her eyes. I knew what she was thinking—she wouldn't have gotten more than one name, if any, outta him. It sucked, but that was the way round here.

"You're right. I've got something else for you," Wallis said. "How about we order some of that chocolate cake and coffee, and I'll get into it then?"

Chapter 16
Abit

AFTER THAT BIG MIDDAY dinner, I followed Della and Alex back to their place. They were already upstairs making coffee. I knew that was a good sign; not letting any dust settle on Wallis's leads.

"He's one of a kind, isn't he, Alex?" I asked. I knew better than to include Della in my question, though that didn't stop her.

"He's a misogynist, is what he is," Della answered. Then she kinda cooled off. "Not that I haven't known hundreds of them on the job. He's actually not the worst I've met, but there is something about him that grates on me. He's the kind of guy you enjoy remembering more than being with. But he did give us some good leads. Thanks to Mister Covington."

"With all due respect to Della and womankind the world over," Alex said, bracing for her comeback, "I like the guy." Della just smiled and took a seat on the couch that looked out over the Black Mountains and a sea of trees.

"That last tidbit he shared over cake and coffee … that was worth it," Della said.

She was talking about what Wade Calhoun and Burt Seely knew of Daisy's disappearance. Seemed back then they'd looked into things more than we'd been led to believe. And Wallis also thought they knew how to find one of Daisy's favorite cousins, though he couldn't remember her name.

We talked for a while over coffee (man, that machine made an amazing brew), but I could tell they were eager to get to work. And Della seemed kinda sidetracked with something else going on. More than oncet lately she and Alex would be talking only to stop kinda sudden-like when I walked into the room.

I said my goodbyes and thanked Alex for picking up the tab. The boys were off to stay with Fiona, so I wouldn't have to do much cooking tonight. Nice change.

I KNEW THOSE TWO would find out more from the cousins, but I wasn't ready to turn the whole investigation over to them. When I got home, I tried googling Burt Seely, but I didn't get far. I wondered how Alex got so deep in his searches. In my mind's eye, I pictured him up in Della's apartment working away, and that led my mind to the house next door, where I grew up and Annie now lived.

Earlier I'd stopped by Coburn's to say howdy when I'd left Della's, but Billie Davis was working, someone I hadn't seen much of since I was a young'un. I recalled why when she scowled at me. I didn't even ask where Annie was, just turned round and shut the door behind me.

It came to me that Annie had been some kind of audio-visual expert with the Raleigh library, and I figured she might be able to help. I got back in my truck and headed to where I'd just left. Kinda crazy, but I was enjoying being free to do exactly what I wanted to do, when I wanted. Of course, I was taking a chance Annie'd be home, not off hiking or hanging out with friends on her day off.

Turned out I found her behind the house, messing round in the old barn. I felt uneasy the way she looked so worried that I'd showed up outta the blue.

"Uh, I was wondering if I could trade you," I said, kicking at the gravel drive.

"Depends on what you're trading ... and asking in return."

"Um, I could help you out here in the barn with, well, whatever you're doing, and maybe you could show me some stuff on the computer. Didn't you do that kinda thing in Raleigh?" I felt sweat slipping down my back, even though it was a chilly day.

She looked round the barn and sighed. "There are some things I want to do out here. I suppose you could help." That made me uneasy, the way she said *suppose*. "But I don't know how much I could show you on the computer, unless you're all thumbs at the keyboard."

No, I wasn't, but some assumptions were hard to get past. At least she didn't say *retard*, like they used to call me. I just nodded at the junk. "We could start with moving this stuff."

Oncet inside the barn, I realized how much crap I'd left after Mama died. I recognized a lot of things Daddy had thrown back there, like the burnt-out potbellied stove and a cheap old dresser. And a table with three legs. As we scrabbled round looking for what else she could get rid of, I found my old chair, left to rot in the back where rain could splash on it. I asked Annie if I could have it.

"It's yours, isn't it?" She musta remembered when her daddy delivered his honey—even my Daddy could sell that fine stuff—and I'd be sitting in the chair, year after year.

While we worked, I asked what she wanted the space for. Surely she wasn't that much of a neatnik that she'd be doing this for no reason.

"I paint some, and the light here is especially good. I've made some glass panes to use when I'm in here with the doors open. That and a space heater should work this time of year."

"I'd like to see your artwork sometime." She just nodded. I reckoned that did sound kinda lame, like something I'd heard in a bad joke.

When we'd finished moving more pieces of junk and I'd demolished the table into kindling, she brushed her hands on her jeans. "Let's go in. I'll make some tea and boot up my laptop."

I loaded the old chair into the truck and headed up the steps to her house. My old house. Oncet there, I felt dizzy. Like I'd never lived there and had stepped into someone else's life. Of course, I *had*. Between Annie and that writer before her, they'd fixed it up nice, painting and decorating in a style way beyond hillbilly poor.

All kinds of memories came flooding back. I thought about the outhouse and how happy we were to get indoor plumbing; Mama seemed cheerful for a week or two. She even hosted her church's Bible group for some coffee and rolls, like for the first and last time, so she could show off our new plumbing. And when I looked up the stairs, I remembered how scared I was of whatever was up there, making strange noises. Our bedrooms were on the first floor, and I'd lay in bed imagining a rocking chair going back and forth, back and forth. It wasn't 'til I was older that I saw a crazy cardinal banging into the glass at his reflection. He'd hit the window—not hard enough to harm himself, just enough to scare *me*—and come back for more. He lived there for years and never did learn he was just fighting with his own self. Like a lot of people, me included.

By the time I left Annie's, I was feeling better. Things had eased up while we worked on her computer. I didn't let on I knew just about everything she'd showed me. I did learn about one site that listed property owners and another that allowed you to do ancestral searches without having to join.

As I drove home, I thought about second chances. Maybe I was due one. I wondered for about the hundredth time why Della had never dated when she and Alex divorced. That ranger, Gregg somebody, was as close as she came. I'd asked her about that not long ago, and she'd said something about women of a certain age didn't have much luck thataway. She'd gone out with a bunch of losers before she'd met Alex, and a few more afterwards while she still lived in D.C. "Alex was the one who got away ... and came back," she'd added, smiling. "I guess that was what I was waiting for."

"The *one*, huh?" I'd asked. "I sure hope we get to have more than that. Fiona's gone now, and though I don't want her back, at the time I was sure she was the one."

"Oh, just let her be one of the ones. Don't put any voodoo on yourself." Then she added outta the blue, "Besides, you and Annie go way back."

"Not sure she's up for anything like that."

"Like what?"

"Well, you know, like my, uh, girlfriend. We're just old friends."

"We'll see."

Chapter 17
Abit

AFTER I UNLOADED MY old chair at the woodshop, I was still full from that big midday dinner at The Rib so I worked through suppertime and into the night. I sanded off years of dirt and hard times (if only it were that easy), followed by tung oil and new inner-tube strips to make the softest seat in the world. That old chair had served me well during a time when I had nothing better to do than to lean against a store. First Daddy's, then Della's.

It cleaned up so nice I thought about putting it somewhere special, but it didn't go with anything in the house. The shop would be fine, a place to take breaks in comfort.

I tripped over Cat when I stood to turn out the woodshop lights. I picked him up, sat back down on my chair, and petted him until we both started to purr. "Yeah, this is a fine old chair, Cat, and you're welcome to sit in it any time you like. When you're not busy catching rats, that is."

As I looked round the moonlit woodshop, it took on a quality I'd never seen before. The tools I'd gathered to make a life for myself seemed to glow with an energy all their own, as if they enjoyed a secret life when I wasn't round. Moonlight danced on my best plane, reminding me of the first thing I'd ever made with it—a cradle for Conor. Me and that plane worked that wood so fine, as though with enough care we could smooth out the life that lay ahead for him.

I set Cat down and put out fresh water before heading to the house. On the way, though it was too dark to see them, I smelled those blamed skunks again, hunting grubs and whatever else they ate of an evening. I reckoned they were nesting under the house, drawn to the heat from the woodstove. I grabbed my flashlight and looked all round the foundation. Eventually I found the hole where they were getting into the cellar.

Over the next coupla days, with some help from Google, I made a one-way door to stick into that hole. Since they slept in the day, I had plenty of time to get it in place. When I'd finished, I felt good they could get out that night, but couldn't get inside come morning.

Good riddance and don't come back!

Chapter 18
Abit

T HE PHONE WOKE ME. I scrambled to grab it before it could ring again, my heart pounding at the thought something bad had happened. Why else would someone be calling this time of night? Then I looked at my bedside clock. Ten o'clock. In the morning. Mollie glanced over, kinda groggy from so much sleep. For the past week I hadn't been sleeping good, so I musta needed it.

"Hello," I croaked.

"WHAT THE FRAK? You feeling okay? It's nearabout noon." Never mind he'd added a coupla hours for effect. Typical of folks round here, suspicious of people who rose after six a.m., even if they'd worked half the night on something important.

"I'm fine, Wallis. What's up?"

"I'm in town. I took your suggestion to heart and used a payphone. I ran into Burt Seely, and he wants to meet with you and Alex. Only when I called Alex, that Kincaid woman said Alex was too busy. We've gotta go now if you want to talk with him."

I told Wallis I'd meet him at Burt's place, which he explained was just north of Newland. On the drive over, I realized I hadn't heard from Alex about getting in touch with Wade Calhoun, that old cousin of Wallis's. I was surprised Alex hadn't jumped on that chance to meet one of the cousins.

Burt's driveway was empty. I'd beaten Wallis there, and I wasn't sure how to handle things. I'd hoped to get a chance to talk with Wallis before we met with Burt, but it didn't look like that was gonna happen.

The house sat just off the dirt road, surrounded by a white-picket fence and a groomed front yard with trimmed boxwood bushes. You'd think that would be a good sign, but I'd found people with front yards that neat often turned out to be ornery.

Burt came out on the porch and waved at me. He stood tall and lean, wiry some would call it. I acted like I had something to do in the truck before I got out. When I couldn't put it off any longer, I opened the truck door and heard Wallis's truck coming down the road. I sighed with relief.

We took advantage of the sunny November day and sat on the porch. Burt or some relative had situated the house so it looked west, perfect for sunsets over the mountains. A wide creek below made its way over rocks and round trees, a setting just made for birds of all kinds. I heard a kingfisher chattering away, inviting some fish to join him for dinner. I coulda sat there all day.

I musta spaced out, drifting along with that creek, because all of a sudden Wallis was shaking my arm. "Abit, Burt here says Dr. Dawson was as fine a man as he'd ever met."

I could feel my face flush, both from getting caught daydreaming as well as the depth of Burt's ignorance. I'd read that diary. I knew what the rest of the world hadn't known about Dr. Dawson. But I just nodded, though not without asking, "Can you think of any reason he'd take little Daisy away from her home?"

"I believe she was mentally ill. Making up lies and such to the point she needed care," Burt said, burping halfway through what sounded like a prepared speech. He liked his stories like his yard: neat and tidy. But I had trouble believing him. No doubt the asylum story had become family lore, passed down generation to generation. I had no way of knowing it then, but I was right to doubt him. Just wrong about why.

"Is there anyone else on your side of the family who might know about Daisy's disappearance?" I asked.

"Maybe," Burt said, rubbing his chin. "But before we go any further, I want to know why you two are so blamed interested in this sad old story."

Fortunately I'd figured we'd get a question like that. "A friend of mine, Della Kincaid, is a journalist, and she's researching some of the unsolved mysteries of the mountains." It'd sounded good when I practiced on Mollie, but now it fell kinda flat, even to my ears.

"Well, it weren't no mystery. I mean, I don't know for sure what happened, but I trust my cousin, Emmet. Dr. Dawson to you."

"You're a good bit younger than him," I pointed out, leaving it hanging out there that maybe he wasn't old enough back in the day to form a trustworthy opinion.

"Old enough to spend time with him at family reunions." He looked over at Wallis. "Your mama was always organizing them, and Emmet was good with us kids. Playing with us when others couldn't be bothered. You know their kind: children should be seen, not heard."

I nodded and looked to Wallis for help keeping the conversation going; I was more interested in the grand view from Burt's porch. All my life I'd heard people claim that local folks saw the mountains more as wallpaper, too used to them to really see their beauty. Well, here was a man who'd put that claim to rest. I could agree with Burt on that.

I snapped back again when I heard Wallis say, "Okay, like young Abit asked, is there anyone else who can shed light on this? What about Wade Calhoun?"

Burt shook his head. "He called me yesterday, said he'd gotten a call from someone who was looking into this. He doesn't want you or anyone else bothering him." (I reckoned Alex had tried after all.) Wallis looked steamed enough that Burt added real quick-like, "What I mean is he said I know everything he knows."

Wallis grunted but didn't say another word. After a time, I finally wrestled outta Burt the name of Daisy's other cousin she liked so well: Darlene Cunningham.

"She's on our side of the family too. Emmet's side. She was like an older sister to Daisy. Lives in Blowing Rock in one of them government housing places for seniors. She's pushing ninety, but still sharp. You'd best be going up there while the going's good."

DARLENE CUNNINGHAM LOOKED LIKE one of those apple-head dolls Mama made come winter, her face all wrinkled and curling in on itself. I'd known a lot of old women who looked thataway, a testament to years of hard work and mountains of sorrow. But she was dressed real nice in black slacks and a floral top, and she hadn't even known we were coming.

When we'd settled in on her couch, she offered us hot coffee and fresh cinnamon rolls. "I didn't make them, but my neighbor did, and I've never tasted anything bad outta that kitchen."

The coffee was hot and strong, and she hadn't lied about those rolls. Not too much icing, but what there was had oozed down into the crevices and mixed with the cinnamon. Darlene's hospitality was the genteel kind, which was why I nearly choked on a bite of roll when she said, "Burt called and said you're here about that turd-wearing-pants Dawson."

"Uh, Burt said he was a fine man," I offered. She just rolled her eyes. "Do you think he did harm to little Daisy?"

"Oh, now there was a sweet girl. I loved her like a sister and missed her when they took her away. I tried to find out where she'd gone, but all anyone would say was Virginie. *For her own good*, as if she'd done something wrong. I never believed that. As for Dr. Dawson, he drank more than a fish. And that kinda behavior usually leads to the no-good kind you're hinting at. Don't listen to Burt. He don't know his backside from a hole in the ground."

All along I'd made no secret of not liking Dr. Dawson, but something about the way Darlene jumped all over him didn't sit right, either. More like she was jealous or resentful. I looked round her apartment, and it was a nice place, at least for those of us not in the *professional* class, so I couldn't understand what had turned her so bitter. Then again, there was no telling what mountain people, fueled by years of grudges, could dream up. We were awfully good at that.

"Do you remember her friend, Amy?" I asked, still hoping we could find her.

"Yes, I can see her clear as day," Darlene said. "A nice girl from a Christian family. I believe they were in the same class at school. But best I recollect, Amy's family moved away not long after Daisy left."

"Do you know Amy's last name?" I asked, one last try.

She thought a minute. "No, Honey, I don't."

After that Wallis asked a few more questions, but Darlene kept repeating herself. When she crossed her arms over her bosom, I motioned for us to go. And just like that, when we stood, she turned real nice again and scurried off to her kitchen to package up some of those rolls for us to take with us. I couldn't say no, and I noticed Wallis's eyebrows going up and down with anticipation of having another one with the next morning's coffee.

I was sincere when I thanked her for her time and hospitality. And, really, for confirming my suspicions. I just couldn't figure out why I felt uneasy. Maybe because her account and Burt's cancelled out one another. It felt like we were getting nowhere fast.

Wallis and I chatted briefly when we got out to our trucks. He thought she'd been more helpful than Burt Seely, and I told him about my concerns. "We haven't cracked it yet, Wallis."

"Well, young Abit, perhaps Alex has found something for us. Just let me know." He tooted his horn and drove off.

I got in my truck and started driving toward Hanging Dog. The boys were home again and needing their supper, and I was grateful for some leftover Brunswick Stew. I'd make cornbread, and we'd go from there.

As I drove, I had a vision of something that could only be from my past, though I'd never remembered anything like it before. I pulled over at the next wide spot and stopped the truck. There was Daddy raging round the house, yelling like a holy terror. Mama was crying, and I'd gotten behind the couch to hide. I figured Darlene's rantings about Dr. Dawson sparked it. I saw Mama run to their bedroom, slamming the door.

I started breathing real sharp, wishing the vision would end. It finally did, but not before Mama was dressed for Sunday services. And that's when lightning finally struck. I got this strong feeling that after Daddy hit her, that was when she joined her crazy church at the VFW. She *needed* them. They supported her. An old saying ran through my head unbidden: *No tongue could tell the sorrow she'd known.*

When I figured the awful memories were over, I got a new one of him throwing me round in a fit of anger. I was just a little feller then, bones not much bigger than a willow branch. I was 4, maybe close to 5 year old because it was spring and my birthday is in June.

I breathed deep for a while until it was safe to drive toward home.

Chapter 19
Della

COBURN'S FELT LONESOME THIS time of year. Early nightfall came down hard, especially stuck inside this place filled with so many memories, good and bad. Times like this reminded me how much I'd struggled during my first years in Laurel Falls, except back then I was fueled by hope. I knew I could make a success of Coburn's, hard times just stepping stones. And I did. Make a success of it. Only now I didn't know what to hope for.

I headed to the back to make a cup of tea. Just when the kettle started to boil, I heard the bell over the door. Wouldn't you know it?

"Hey, Della, you back there?"

Abit. Couldn't have asked for a better interruption. I put more tea in the pot and added water to the kettle.

"Let's celebrate and open some of those new confections I ordered from that bakery in Asheville," I said. "Eccles cakes. When I saw them on their latest order sheet, I remembered they were a favorite of Nigel's." (Nigel Steadman was an old friend of both Abit's and mine, but he'd returned to England when he'd caused so many problems he'd worn out his welcome. Even so, I missed him.)

"What are we celebrating? Not that I'm questioning your idea," Abit said, already reaching for one of the cakes filled with currants and spices.

"Oh, I don't know. Do we need a reason?" When he just shrugged, I added, "That you showed up just when I was bored out of my skull."

"Man, these are good. What are Eccles cakes, anyway?"

I knew what they tasted like, but I didn't know much about their origins. Like so many British goodies, they often had a fascinating history. I checked the package.

"Ha! Listen to this: *Eccles cakes have been popular since at least the 17th century, until the Puritans banned them for being too indulgent and tempting to the soul, even causing revelry!* No wonder I pulled those out today. I need some revelry. Oh wait, it goes on to say that Oliver Cromwell threatened imprisonment for anyone caught eating one. We'd better hope Sheriff Horne doesn't stop by and arrest us."

"More like eat 'em all up," Abit said with his mouth full, reveling in the temptation.

"So what's on your mind?"

"What, I can't just stop by?" He acted all innocent, but I could tell he had something to share. "Wallis and I went to see Burt Seely and Darlene Cunningham—Daisy's cousins."

"Hey, I thought we were going together."

"Wallis knew Burt Seely, and when he called, Burt said we needed to go right away."

That's when I remembered Wallis *had* called early that morning. I'd answered and relayed Wallis's request to Alex, who'd said he was too busy to drop everything at such short notice. "Have you noticed that Wallis has some kind of grudge against me? And a bromance going with Alex?" Abit laughed, which was the best remedy for my pout. "Speaking of whom, Alex did find something he wanted me to report. But you first."

Abit brought me up to date about Daisy allegedly going to Virginia, something I promised to look into, though to be honest, that wasn't much to go on. Then he mentioned the dueling cousins. "It was kinda strange. Burt loved the doctor, Darlene hated his guts. Seemed like a wash to me and Wallis."

"Don't be too discouraged," I said, stifling a smile. Abit always looked so dejected when things went like this. "At least now we know Dr. Dawson wasn't all bad."

"I'm not really that upset about those two cousins. It was something else that happened." I waited. "I got these visions, or maybe more like flashbacks, that came to me after Darlene carried on so about what a mean drunk the doctor was."

I kicked myself for assuming his sorrow was about something sixty years in the past. I poured him more tea and pushed the plate of Eccles cakes closer. He shook his head—a sure sign he felt bad. When he was through sharing, I couldn't think of anything to say other than facile bromides, so I just held his hand. We sat like that until the bell over the door rang.

Chapter 20
Abit

Every time I thought I was over all those troubles from when I was a boy, something happened to bring them up again. But at least this time it felt like I was getting closer to the center of that onion—the way my counselors at The Hicks described the layers of life.

By the time I finally made it home, the sun had slipped behind the mountains, only its purple and pink flames keeping the night at bay. Even the swallows had gone to bed. The boys ran out to greet me, and my cares seemed to go the way of the day.

After dinner, we played a game of Monopoly. Oncet they'd headed to their room to finish homework and get ready for bed, I pulled out my notes and recalled Della saying she and Alex had found something. Me and my troubles had pushed all that aside. I picked up the phone.

"Feeling better?" Della asked when she answered. It still surprised me when people knew who was calling.

"About some things. But feeling bad I never asked what you and Alex uncovered."

"Oh well, you are now. That's the way it works sometimes. I've been trying to pull everything together from this crazy investigation, but it's all scrambled."

"Same here. All we know is what the diary already told us: Daisy was in trouble. And that she stopped writing all sudden-like. Her parents both sounded awful, but by my calculations the father was the meanest."

"Okay, we've been round and round about that," Della said. "We'll need—for now—to agree to disagree. One way or another, Daisy left the household. But she wasn't the only one. I've been thinking about how strange it was that both of Daisy's siblings also disappeared once they finished their schooling. That doesn't feel right."

"Yeah, but families branch out in different directions, though I'm not sure that was so common back then. But if the family was a mess, her brother and sister coulda just left to get a clean start. Little Daisy didn't get that chance. And I don't believe the cousins who say she went to a loony bin. Her writing in the diary just didn't sound crazy."

Della agreed. "More likely what you said earlier—family lore passed down, growing more distorted with each iteration."

"And don't forget the two cousins on the father's side who were a draw. One loving him, the othern hating him."

"That's where Alex and my news comes in. We worked on finding out more about Dr. Dawson through some medical licensing websites and talking with a few retired doctors who'd worked with him. To a person, they loved the guy. The only thing we found derogatory was a couple of leaves of absence so he could go to rehab. As we already knew, alcohol had gotten a hold on him."

"I still don't trust him," I said, digging in my heels. She ignored that, which was as good as saying she didn't agree. "Speaking of alcohol," I went on, "I've worked out why Mama needed that church of hers. I've always been critical about those folks—they treated me like I were a freak—but they musta given her something she needed. Friendship and hope."

"Same goes for Vester. Not the church part, but the hopeless part. You told me he quit drinking when you were born ..."

"I'm not so sure that's true," I interrupted. "Those flashbacks put the lie to that."

"Whatever, when I met him years later, he had given up alcohol, but he was still troubled, living on the edge. I know dry drunks. Not that my parents ever got dry, but I've met quite a few over the years, and they're a mess. They guzzle spirits because their spirit is broken, but when they give up the spirits, they still haven't healed their own spirit. It's a vicious circle."

I hated to disagree with Della, but I wasn't ready to give drunks—dry or wet—much leeway. I gritted my teeth and said a passable goodbye before hanging up.

THAT NIGHT I TOSSED and turned while Mollie snored next to me. I couldn't hold with Della letting drunks off the hook thataway. They should be held accountable for all the hurt they cast upon everyone round them.

I just lay there forever, staring at the ceiling with dark thoughts filling my head. After a while, the knotty-pine patterns in the wood played tricks on my eyes. I could see all kinds of people up there: some plowing, others sowing, all of them working hard at life, trying to keep tough times away. And then unbidden I saw what Della was talking about. Sure enough, when their spirit got low, they reached for the easy kind in a bottle and lost their footing.

I turned over and hugged my dog.

You'd think notions like that would've kept me awake the rest of the night, but I'd lived those old stories for a long, troubling time. These new thoughts, offering an unfamiliar sense of acceptance, lulled me to sleep.

Chapter 21
Abit

THE NEXT DAY I drove the boys to school, where Fiona would pick them up later for a long weekend in Asheville. Fortunately they didn't need to carry grips with underwears and clothes and such; they had extras down there.

When I got home, I headed to my shop, put the coffee on, and fooled round with an order. I always felt untethered right after the boys left for a visit with their mother. Fears, warranted or not, blew in like a cold wind outta nowhere.

I was reaching for my second cup when I saw someone driving toward the house. I didn't recognize the car—a late model of some kind, which you didn't see much round here.

A man dressed in a three-piece suit got out. His hair perfectly groomed, kinda like those TV evangelists. Or a lawyer. I could see Sparky taking notice too, sitting on his haunches, wondering like me what kind of trouble had just pulled in.

"Hello, Abit," he said smiling. "Glad to see your old friend?"

I still didn't know who he was. Until he saluted. That was something he used to do, just being silly, because there was no way Shiloh was ever in the military.

"Did your father-in-law dress you this morning?" I asked, grinning like a fool at seeing my old woodworking partner after what? At least a coupla year.

"Hey, Charlene and I aren't married," he said, holding up his ringless left hand for proof. "And no, her father didn't have anything to do with my attire. Other than the salary he pays me." He twirled to show off the fine cut of his clothes.

I'd met Shiloh at The Hicks, where he learned to make fine dovetail joints and finish furniture with a patience I didn't have. That was a special time in my life when I first learned about fellowship round the dinner table and helping folks do their best work, not tearing them down outta spite. I didn't understand it at the time, but I'd been longing for that my whole life. Until then I'd never experienced anything like that, but somehow I musta known deep down, with some help from Jesus, that life called on us to do right by one another.

After we'd left school, Shiloh and I worked together five or six year. Then he left with Charlene, who seemed more stable than his previous string of girlfriends. And it didn't hurt she had a hotshot father who owned some kinda conglomerate and had money to burn. Shiloh had been our resident Zen guy, always dressed in baggy pants and loose shirts and reeking of patchouli. To be honest, I was having trouble connecting the two, the one in my memory and the one before my eyes. And he knew it.

"Hard to believe, eh, Abit?" he said, laughing and holding his arms out. Around these parts we'd say he looked prissy, all decked out like that. He was built kinda slight, and that finely tailored suit made him look even more so. "The Old Man sent me on a sales trip to Charlotte, and I couldn't head back to D.C. without stopping to see you."

It was cold out, so I motioned for us to head inside my shop. As I was getting Mollie back in, Shiloh seemed to take notice of all the half-finished projects gathering dust.

"Your shop looks like that butcher's who backed into his meat grinder," he said. "You know, the one who got a little behind in his work?" He loved those corny old jokes, and I had to admit, it felt good to laugh. "You need a hand?" he added.

"Missing the old life?" I asked, just joking. He didn't answer. Then again, what was here to miss? After an awkward pause, I added, "Let's go to the house and have some dinner. You ready for something to eat, or are you watching your figure?"

His turn to laugh. Seemed to have loosened up some since the last time I saw him. Of course that was when Fiona had just left, and I was a mess. He'd been a good friend and helped get out orders when I couldn't.

"Just what is it you do to earn those fancy duds? And car?" I asked, nodding my head toward what I now saw was a 2012 Lexus.

"You know how mindfulness is *the* trending word these days?" I didn't, but I nodded. "The Old Man saw that I could teach that to the corporate types in his enterprise. Turns out I'm a good teacher. For all our disagreements, Abit, you always did say I had the patience of Job."

"Well, it does look like you got twicet as much as you had before." He looked confused so I told him about the Bible saying that about Job. "It's like everything you did here was leading toward your real purpose in life."

"Not quite. My work here was important too. But yes, life is a continuum. Wherever we go, there we are."

"Yes, and the sun rises and sets each day," I sniped. He always could get under my skin with that guru stuff, but I caught myself before I said anything else. Why put a damper on good times now?

Then he had to go and say, "Oh, I like that. May I use that in my seminars?"

Shiloh hung round for a while, and I kept thinking he was about to say he needed to go. Not that I wanted him to, but in the past, he'd always been scuttling off to be by himself so he could meditate. Now he seemed to be enjoying his trip down memory lane.

After a time, he asked if he could spend the night. I couldn't figure why he hadn't lined up that fancy bed-and-breakfast down the road since he was surely on an expense account, but I was happy for the company. With the boys away, the long winter nights hung heavy. I'd been finding occasional loneliness a difficult companion. If you lived alone long enough, like I did come summer when the boys were down in Asheville so long, you learned how to roll with it. But if it came on you every other weekend, when your life had been filled with talk and laughter and music, it weighed on you.

I pulled some spaghetti sauce outta the freezer, then stopped. "This has meat in it, Shiloh. Not a lot, but I can make something with eggs instead. And by the way, do your corporate types call you Shiloh or Bob? Or Mr. Greene?"

"Eggs would be great, and Shiloh works well with the mindfulness training."

Of course it did.

AFTER DINNER, WE SAT close by the wood heater. We'd been having a spell of awful low temperatures, and the house creaked with cold. We were on our second beer when he asked, "Is there anything I can help you with?"

"You mean in the shop?" I asked, confused about where he was headed.

"No, I'm not dressed to help out there, but I've got a fast laptop, and I've acquired computer skills you wouldn't believe."

"Well, dang if I don't," I said, grateful for an unexpected favor.

He plugged in his laptop, and quick as I told him things about Daisy and Emmet, he plowed somewhere deep in the Internet. And sure enough, he came up with a lead we hadn't thought of. I couldn't wait to tell Della.

Chapter 22
Della

"Stop digging, or you'll be digging your own grave."

Someone had slipped a note through the slot in Coburn's front door. I was glad it was my turn to open the store so Annie didn't find the threat. She was even more superstitious than Abit.

The next day, I raced from my apartment—before my coffee, even—in hopes of intercepting any new threats. Nothing at the front door. I consoled myself that it was just a one-off, likely after a drinking binge. But when I logged onto the store computer, an email included a crude drawing of a noose. Later, a letter in the U.S. mail featured a cut-and-paste note with dead animals surrounded by swastikas. The sensibilities of whoever was behind these threats were all over the place. They reminded me of the Green Treatise militia from that first summer Abit and I worked a caper together. We'd thought they'd drifted away, but more than likely they'd gone underground and festered.

Hard to figure who might be behind these, though it had to be someone connected to the Dawson family. Abit and I hadn't shared much about the diary or our research, even with Wallis and Annie. But of course the people we'd interviewed were abuzz on Laurel Falls' impressive grapevine, and someone must have gotten his back up. Family secrets were sacrosanct around here.

That afternoon, I was upstairs doing the books when Abit knocked on the door. When I opened up, he skipped hello and blurted out, "Hey, guess who came to see me?"

It must have been someone good because he looked awfully pleased with himself. "Annie?" I said, attributing his jubilance to that side of his life.

His face fell. "Er, no. Shiloh."

"I didn't think you'd be so glad to see him."

"He grew on me, especially back when he helped me out. And he's helped us out again. He thought of something I hadn't considered. Maybe you hadn't either."

"So Shiloh's a detective now?"

"No, a computer whiz. Hacker, to be honest. He learned all this stuff working for his girlfriend's father. And you wouldn't recognize him. I didn't at first. Thought he was a TV preacher." He laughed again, and this time I joined him. That was quite a picture. "He pulled out his laptop and hacked into some records—I didn't want to know too much about what he was doing—and discovered Daisy's brother is still alive. Wallis had heard he'd died, but maybe that's because they didn't know what his name was."

"Isn't it Dill Dawson?"

"So you would think. And yes, it *was*. Until he changed it." Abit was stretching this out on purpose. Just when I was feeling the first tendrils of irritation, he added, "He goes by Dawson Dillard now. And *he* seems to be the one with mental problems."

According to Abit, Dill/Dawson was living somewhere in the region, though even Shiloh couldn't find an address or contact information. What he did find was that Dill/Dawson had been housed in some kind of rehab center for a while, but was released when funds for social services were cut. The report said the powers that be had determined he was lucid enough to live on his own.

I turned to my computer and started checking. No luck. I couldn't find anything more recent, either. He probably was living rough or completely off the grid. I couldn't find anything new.

But in a small town, you didn't necessarily need a computer. Eyes and ears were always to the ground. We headed downstairs.

Annie was restocking shelves when we went inside. Abit went all nervous, greeting her with a near whisper and flushed face. I was grateful I didn't have his red-hair complexion; it gave away too much. I'd never have pulled off so many bluffs back in the day.

I explained what we needed, and Annie said she'd ask around. I told her both names, mentioning that Dawson Dillard was his latest. Then I left Abit down there to do whatever he could with that situation.

BY THE TIME ALEX came home, I felt lower than low.

"I'm slipping," I told him.

"On the ice? It's freezing out there," he said as he took off his coat and scarf and boots. He'd been in the higher mountains hiking with a friend from the magazine. He set a white bag on the counter.

"No, I said *slipping*. Not *slipped*."

"Okay, Editor-in-Chief, what's up?"

I told him about the Dawson brother. "Back in my prime, I would have caught something like that. At least done some research on different names."

"Don't be hard on yourself, Della."

"No, I'd've spotted that."

"Well, you got it now."

"No, I didn't get it. Shiloh got it."

Alex started laughing, but the look on my face stopped him. He came over and hugged me. "You're just jealous that a patchouli-stinking twit beat you to something."

"According to Abit, he wears a three-piece suit now and drives a Lexus." I looked down at myself. "I'm wearing a two-piece track suit and drive a twenty-year-old Jeep."

"I'll get you some patchouli for Christmas," Alex said, putting his arm around me and ushering me toward the kitchen. He opened the white sack and took out six scones.

I put the kettle on.

Chapter 23
Della

I WASN'T EXPECTING ANNIE to uncover much. After all, she lived only sixteen mossy steps from the store and best I could tell, didn't get out much, especially during dark November evenings. But when I went down to the store the next day, she was beaming.

I chuckled and walked over to her, pretending to take a leaf from around her ear. "Had your ear to the ground, eh?"

She put her hand up to her ear and started fanning. "And it's burning!"

"Let me get the coffee on, then *I'm* all ears."

Once we'd settled, me at the register and Annie on the old-folks chair next to it, she said, "Daddy has seen Dawson around doing odd jobs. He even hired him to help with the bees. He must be a good worker because Daddy wouldn't let just anyone do that." I nodded. Elbert would never do anything to jeopardize the quality of his sourwood honey. "Daddy said he drives an old Chevy truck. 1965 or so. Black. Not so many of those on the roads these days, even with folks hanging onto their trucks longer. There aren't any plates on it, but with the sheriff stationed in Newland, that doesn't seem to be a problem."

A customer came in and Annie grumbled under her breath. "Hold on a minute, Della," she whispered. "I've got something really good to share."

I did a little paperwork before the customer came over to check out. I didn't know him—I really should spend more time down here—so we talked about the weather (cold but sunny) and the upcoming Thanksgiving holiday (just a week away). When the bell on the front door signaled his departure, Annie came back to her chair.

"Okay, what's the good news?" I asked.

"Daddy and I were talking, and an idea popped into my head. I asked him if Dawson—he never knew him as Dill, a name Abit mentioned—showed up presentable when he helped with the bees. 'Absolutely,' he said. 'Looked fine.'" Annie did a spot-on impersonation of Elbert. She stopped and looked at me, as though I should understand what that meant. I made a go-on motion with my hand. "Well, he must clean his clothes somewhere, and he doesn't seem to have any relatives nearby, so my guess would be he uses Blanche's machines. And if he goes there, she'll know all about him and where he lives. Probably all his scars or tattoos too."

I chuckled. That might have been the first joke I'd ever heard from Annie. But then a wave of dread came over me at the prospect of putting up with Blanche Scoggins, our ornery launderess, for the possibility of a tidbit of information. I thanked Annie and went upstairs to think more about this. Or, rather, find my courage.

I called Abit on the off chance he might go with me. I dreaded facing Blanche alone.

"What?" he asked. "No way, Della. You know I'd help if I could, but I just can't put myself in front of that woman. Ever again. Sorry. I'll take you to lunch afterwards, I'll mop the store floor for a month, almost anything other than going to Blanche's."

Poor guy. Blanche turned mean as a snake at just the sight of him. We wouldn't get anything out of her with all that animosity in the air. Not that I was exempt from her vitriol.

"WELL, LOOKY THERE. MISS Fancy Washer, what brings you into *my* laundry?" Blanche barked when I came through her double doors.

Some greeting, though to be fair, I hadn't been to the Wash 'n' Swear (aka Wash 'n' Wear) for ages. But I was taken aback that she knew about my new washer. What kind of gossip mill cared about something like that?

"I need some information, Blanche." No point in niceties. She'd be crabby whether I shared them or not.

"Figures. You're on one of your ... what does that strange boy call them, capers? And you expect me to help you with it?"

"First, Blanche, let's get it straight once and for all. His name is Abit, not *strange boy* or any of your other derogatory terms for him. He's never done anything to you, so give him a break. And he's a *man*, for crying out loud."

"Well, Missy, you're not off to a good start if you're expecting any help from me." She crossed her arms over her chest and stared.

"Yeah, well, you owe me, Blanche, and it's time to pay up."

She acted like she didn't know what I was talking about, but we both knew I'd helped keep her out of jail all those years ago. I just stared back at her, and she finally broke down.

"That was twenty-five year ago."

"But you never made amends with me, and I kept my mouth shut about your involvement—even if only tangentially—in those crimes."

"Oh, you and your big words. Ask your questions and get out. And then we're even." She raised her eyebrows, waiting for confirmation that this was the last time I could play that card.

I nodded and asked about Dill Dawson and Dawson Dillard. Turned out she knew him by the latter.

"He cleans his clothes—more like rags, if you ask me—and he's quiet and polite. Not like those kids who come in after school to wash their athletic gear."

"What does he drive? Where does he live?"

"Some beat-up Chevy truck. I'd say about 1962, '63." When I looked at her funny, she chuckled. A rare site. "Oh, I know my trucks. As to where he lives, he talked about out Hanging Dog way. Isn't that where that, uh, *Abit* lives?"

I ignored her question. She didn't really want an answer. After that, I didn't get much more out of her, just the fact he'd mentioned Gumlog Road. That *was* near Abit's farm.

When I got back to the store, Annie was in a tizzy. She held out a crumpled piece of notebook paper. Another threat from the cousins or whoever was behind them. It was time to do something about that.

Chapter 24
Abit

THE NEXT MORNING, I sat alone in the quiet house, hunched up close to the fire. I had a coupla orders calling to me, and of course, my new mandolin was crying for attention. After my early worries, I was actually feeling pretty good about its finer points. Like the neck I'd carved and the way it attached to the fretboard. Not a bad job on the heel of the neck, either, especially with the near-perfect transition to where it met the instrument's body.

But I thought of my workshop in that cold barn and shivered. I'd give the sun more time to warm things up.

As I did my breakfast dishes, my thoughts drifted to, what else, Daisy—where she'd ended up in 1948 and where she was now. We knew somebody took her somewhere, but after all the research and fuss, that was about all we knew. Her family on both sides was all mixed up about who they loved and who they hated. Seemed like nobody knew what had become of her brother Dill, and I hadn't heard a peep about Daisy's baby sister.

Maybe Wallis had a few ideas about where to look next. I planned to make time later to go out his way.

I stood to grab my old mando so I could play a little tune before I started work. I liked to lose myself in the music, something not all that different from Shiloh's meditation. Afterwards, I often found I had answers I needed, about more than just music. Same with writing music, though lately I hadn't felt the spark I needed to get the notes and words right.

I stepped over to the corner of the living room where I kept it—not too close to the fire, not too far from the heat—but it wasn't there. I musta played some before bed.

But no sign of it in the bedroom. Or anywhere in the house.

My heart raced as I tore through every room for a second time. Mollie even got worked up, following me round like it were a game, 'til she realized it weren't. We raced out to the woodshop, but no luck there, either. I went back to the kitchen for some coffee (my nerves didn't need it, but my brain did), and that was when I noticed a small hole cut in the glass in the back door. Right above the lock. Why hadn't I felt the cold when I made my coffee—or noticed the smell seeping in from those skunks? I may have closed them out of the cellar, but they still roamed freely outside, tilling up my yard every night looking for grubs. Whatever happened here last night musta stirred them up good.

But they were the least of my worries. Fiona would be like dealing with a hundred skunks if I couldn't find that family instrument.

I did what I always did when something went wrong: I called Della. I told her about the mando, and she surprised me when she said she wasn't surprised. For a minute I thought she'd come out and taken it for Fiona. Or she'd heard Fiona had been out here. But just as fast, I knew that was crazy thinking. Fiona was with the boys. The boys. I felt sick to my stomach as I wondered if Fiona had gotten Conor to bring the mando with him that weekend? Sneaking it out, right under my nose? My heart broke in so many pieces for so many reasons I couldn't speak. I was lost in that misery when I heard Della squawking on the phone. Then the dial tone.

I was still sitting by the fire, holding the phone, when Della drove up. She hurried in and gave me a big hug. "I know what you're thinking, Honey, but you didn't give me a chance to tell you. There was a rash of burglaries over the weekend. Alex's car was broken into, and they stole a stereo he'd just had installed. And you know my new flat-screen TV? Gone."

Della flinched when I started laughing, kinda hysterical-like. "What's going on Abit? Why is that funny? When I walked in you looked like you'd just lost your best friend."

"I thought I had, Della. I'm real sorry about Alex's stereo and your TV. And my mando.

But compared to thinking my boy had snuck that mando back to his mother, well, they don't seem so bad." Della still looked kinda peeved, so I added, "And I'm fixing to find that mando—along with your stuff too. I don't know how yet, but I will."

Chapter 25
Abit

DELLA WAITED FOR ME to calm down before telling her news about Dill Dawson. I liked hearing that Annie had been so helpful.

"I don't think the Dawson clan is behind the burglaries, but I still think it's odd that the three of us—you, me, Alex—had things stolen," she said. "I haven't heard about any other thefts, but we can't rule them out. Let's go see Dill or Dawson or whatever he calls himself now. He doesn't live far from here."

"Is that why you came out here?" I asked. She frowned so big I added quick-like, "Never mind. I should have known better. But I need to find that mando. The Dawsons will have to wait."

"Come with me now, and Alex and I both will help you find your mandolin, I promise. I'll talk with Sheriff Horne. I'll put up a poster in the store. I'll even talk with Blanche again. But for now, let's go find this Dawson character."

WE WOUND THROUGH HANGING Dog, such as it was, and found the shed-like structure Annie had described to Della. Round these parts it was what we called *a coffin ready-made*—a strong wind could have taken it down, with him in it. We spotted his beat-up 1963 Chevy truck in the drive.

Della knocked softly on the door; its hinges wouldn't take more pressure than that. "Mr. Dillard? It's Della Kincaid and Abit Bradshaw. We've come to talk to you about something we found that belongs to your family." We heard grumbling behind the door, but no effort to open it. "Please. We'd like to talk to you. I'll pay you for your time."

When the door opened a crack, an old man looked out, squinting his eyes in the bright light. Only a dull, yellow glow from an oil lamp shone behind him in the windowless shed. But his appearance wasn't as rough as I'd expected. His white beard had been neatly trimmed, and what I could see of his shirt looked clean.

"Who did you say you were?"

"Abit Bradshaw," I said, stepping closer. "I found your sister's diary and want to return it. We're trying to find her."

"No idea what's become of them," he said. "She disappeared one day and left us. Mama and I had to look after the family. Daddy was a drunk. Not a mean one, just drank too much. Like I do." He stopped to cough, and the acrid smell of stale alcohol came off his breath in waves. "No, I haven't heard from Violet or Daisy in a good fifty year," he continued after spitting out something I managed to look away in time to miss. "We've lost touch. Like we don't even know one another." He sighed and held out his arms, straight like a scarecrow. "Then again, look at me—why would anyone want to know me?"

Neither one of us knew what to say after that. Della reached out and took his hand. "Thank you for your time, Mr. Dillard," slipping him what looked like a couple of twenties.

We hurried to the Jeep—it'd started raining pretty hard—and didn't say a word 'til we reached the tarmac. (It's awful hard to talk on a washboard dirt road.) Della turned left toward home. After a while, she said, "Well, that was sad. And our search seems to be at a dead end. We've found Dill, don't know where Violet is, and we're not one lick closer to Daisy."

"I don't hold with that, Della. I'm still planning to figure this whole mess out."

"Well, good for you," she said not unkindly, more like concerned. After a while she asked, "Why do you care so much?"

"I don't know," I said at first. But then I realized I *did* know. "What's the point of being alive if we don't help one another when we're called to? I know I can't change the world, but I can help those I meet along the way. How could I claim to be a Christian and not extend my hand to someone in need?"

"But no one is asking you to do this."

I shrugged my shoulders and sunk down in the seat. "Della, I just can't turn my back on this. I have to know what happened to Daisy, to make sure she made it through, like I did. Something is calling to me."

"Honey, I doubt she's even alive."

"She could be ... she's not that much older than you."

Della chuckled, though she didn't sound all that happy. "Yeah, you're right, though you're off by ten or more years. But even if she's alive, she could've moved to California. Or Ireland."

"Let's take it one day at a time," I said.

"Hey, that's my line."

"Yeah, you taught me well."

Della smirked. "Okay, but on this one day I can't help but question if it's a good idea to keep searching. What's left to try?"

"Lost your fire, Della? I'm not used to you being Doubting Thomas. Make up your mind. Are you up for this or do you want me to make you a rocking chair?"

That time she laughed for real.

Chapter 26
Abit

I'D TALKED A GOOD story with Della, but by later that day I wasn't so sure I had the time or the spirit to keep this search going, either. Especially with the missing mando eating away at me. I needed to check into all that, finish the new mando, and get ready for Christmas with the boys. It was my year to have them, and I was determined it was gonna be the best one ever.

I drove over to see Wallis, who I figured could help on several fronts. One, I enjoyed the guy's company. Two, he might've heard about the burglaries and any gossip surrounding them. And three, he may have done more research.

I was relieved to see his truck in the drive, but when I knocked on the door, no one answered. I got worried all over again and called out.

"Out here, young Abit," he shouted from what I assumed was a backyard. I'd never paid any mind to the rest of his home—just Wallis, strong coffee, and even stronger opinions.

"WHAT IN THE SAM HILL brought you out here?" I was too struck by his backyard scene to answer. "Well, what?" he nearabout shouted, like I was hard of hearing.

Wallis was dressed in a blue and white pinstriped apron, tending a flock of chickens and talking real nice. Calling them by names like they were young'uns. "Earline, here's some feed for you. Don't let Mildred get it all."

"Hey, that was my mama's name."

"Well, she didn't have a copyright on it," he grumbled, ornery as ever.

"You could at least talk as nice to me as you do your chickens."

"Oh, don't get your FUR A-FLYING," Wallis said, throwing out another handful of corn.

As I watched the chickens hopping and flapping to get their dinner, something caught my eye. Over by the coop, the round opening for the chickens to get in and out was framed by an old toilet seat. He'd propped the lid open so it stuck straight out to give the chickens a little shelter from the rain and snow as they ventured in or out of their coop. I started laughing as I thought about how, with enough space, there was no need to throw anything away.

Even Wallis was chuckling as he untied his apron and headed to the house. "I'm glad you stopped by. You've saved me a trip to town. To call you. Thanks to a lucky coincidence I found another family member who still has enough of his marbles to recall when that young Daisy went away. He told me that her daddy took her to live with a cousin. He didn't know her last name or where she lived, just that Daisy was gone after that. You were right about her not going to the loony bin. But that cousin was on her father's side, so I'm sorry to say I'm give out of clues."

For some reason Daisy's first entry in the diary had stuck in my mind: *I love you, new diary! Thank you, Cousin Evie, for the perfect Christmas present.* I got a shiver, knowing we were onto something. "Della said she was give out too, but I need to get shed of this diary. Have you heard anything about her sister, Violet?"

"No one seems to know about her, neither. She didn't disappear like Daisy, though apparently she moved away. As soon as she could, I reckon."

I started thinking the worst about Daisy's fate. Wallis studied my face and took pity on me.

"Don't go making up bad stories, young Abit. We don't know. I suspect if something truly untoward had happened to that poor girl, someone in my family would have come out with it. Like I've said before—they wouldn't have let that rest. But if you need to get that sorrowful diary off your hands, you can bring it over here, and we'll have a little ceremony with the chickens. Then burn it in my incinerator."

I shook my head, not ready to give in. I waited a beat before mentioning the burglaries and asking what he knew. "Just what you've probably heard. I didn't know they'd taken that glorious mandolin of yours. What sorry SONS OF A

BISCUIT." He took a closer look at me and added, "Now go on home and get some rest. You're starting to look rough." He patted me on the back and handed me a dozen eggs.

I didn't have the heart to tell him I had my own chickens.

I NEVER GOT TO taste those eggs. While I was driving home, I noticed another pickup in my rearview mirror. Not noteworthy in these parts, until he bashed his bigger truck against my bumper. My truck swerved onto the shoulder, but I yanked the steering wheel in time to get it back on the road before he could try again. He let me get on ahead of him, and I let out a sigh of relief. The only damage was a dozen eggs all over my bench seat and dash. *Just some drunk filled with rage*, I thought. But then it came to me. I knew this road and what lay ahead—steep drop-offs with no guard rail or shoulder. He was setting me up.

I heard his truck roar up on me, pulling round so he could drive side by side, edging me into the gulch below. As I struggled with my steering wheel, I caught a glimpse of his face. No one I knew—or wanted to know—but I saw a wicked smile as he worked his steering wheel to the right toward me. The road was just wide enough for the two of us, but with him easing me over, I didn't stand a chance.

When I'd seen this kinda thing on TV, I'd always wondered what would happen if the vehicle in trouble just stopped. The bad guy would be barreling along and have to turn round, which on a road like this would take at least five K-turns. And I didn't know if it were wishful thinking, but I didn't believe this guy would have the guts to stop, get outta his truck, walk back, and stand face-to-face with his prey. Me. He'd stay in the safety of six tons of steel.

Stopping was a risk, but so was driving on.

So I stopped.

Sure enough, the truck went on past me at high speed. We'd kicked up a mess of dust, and I could barely make out his truck, though I did see its brake lights come on. I locked my doors, and threw the truck in reverse, craning my neck over my shoulder to maneuver the truck round a sharp bend in the road. I kept on in reverse, not counting on any common sense from him. If he'd just wanted to scare me, well, he'd accomplished that. His job was done. But if he wanted to kill me, I didn't have a plan for that.

After what felt like forever, and still no sign of him, I took a deep breath, backed the truck onto a wide shoulder, and turned it toward home. I'd've rather stayed put and let my heart slow, but I couldn't risk it. I drove off at a reasonable speed.

All the way home, I kept checking my mirror, but all I saw was my own face, pale and scared.

I did manage a whisper of a chuckle when I recalled something Fiona's father used to say at times like this: *Good job I wore my brown pants.*

Chapter 27
Abit

BACK HOME, I CHECKED my truck all over. Turned out I felt more banged up than it was. I relaxed a little knowing my friend Duane Dockery was good at making dents disappear, but I was on my own when it came to getting myself back together.

I sat a while, my knees all wobbly oncet I was home safe, and thought about how we now knew one thing for certain: someone had followed me to Wallis's place—be that a cousin, brother, or sister of Daisy's—who wanted family secrets to stay secret.

Wallis and Della were probably right that it was time to let this go, but I felt uneasy leaving everything unsolved. Then again, it all happened such a long time ago, what did it matter? I reckoned I just wanted to know that Daisy's life had had a happier ending, like mine had.

As I walked to the house, Mollie and Red came charging up to meet me, paws covered in mud. At least somebody had had a good day. I played with them in the last of the daylight and set out their supper. I looked down toward Matthew's but saw no lights on yet. It would have been a good evening for company.

Instead, I called Della to tell her about the truck chase.

She sighed real big. "This has got to stop." That was when she told me about all the threats that had been coming to the store. She added that they'd upset Annie too. "Two can play at this," was all she said before hanging up.

After that, I headed to the woodshop to finish my mando. Might as well; I'd lost my appetite, a rare occurrence. And I no longer had an instrument to play.

I'd been putting off the next step because it involved the F holes, which really worried me. Hard to finagle them just right. After a few cups of coffee, several ear and belly rubs for Mollie, and half-hearted efforts at cleaning my shop, I couldn't think of any other excuses. I set my fears aside and did the best I could. By the end, I felt like my efforts just may have worked.

That left something called tap tuning, which involved carving the instrument's top and back thicknesses to get the best tone from the soundboard. It was painstaking work, carving away a little wood, tapping on the top and listening for the tone. Then taking off a bit more—but not too much. I was pretty good at carving bears and shotguns, so maybe I could pull this off.

But I decided to leave that for another day, along with Daisy and her diary. I had something even more important to tend to.

Chapter 28
Abit

Della and Alex arrived early for Conor's sixteenth birthday, just a few days before Thanksgiving. I needed some help, so I put them to work in the kitchen. I felt all jittery, worked up about the surprise I had waiting for Conor.

I'd mentioned he could invite any of the boys from his school, but he'd said there was a *girl* he wanted to come. I felt like a fool for not thinking of that. When I asked if she was the same one he'd given his twenty dollar, he mumbled something that sounded like yes.

Turned out Crystal was a quiet girl with dark hair and bright coloring. I could tell Conor was happy she'd come. Vern had his best friend, Lyle, over, a kid he'd palled around with ever since coming to live with us.

For the week before Conor's birthday, I'd played down the day, and wouldn't you know it? I reckoned that tipped Conor off that something big was gonna happen. He was all full of himself, kidding round with me and kinda flirting with Crystal.

Everything was going along fine until Duane Dockery pulled up. Just like a teenager, Conor switched his mood in a flash. "This is *my* party," he squawked, all huffy as Duane parked his truck.

"Well, yes, but it's *my* house." That had been one of Daddy's favorites, and something I'd sworn I'd never say. "I wanted *my* friend here too. You didn't mind that Della and Alex came—with presents, I might add."

"Yeah, but I never liked Duane."

"Why not?"

"I don't know. He just doesn't feel like one of *us*."

I was ashamed of my boy at that moment, but I let it go. It was his day. Still, I was glad Duane had come, for reasons Conor would soon see.

In spite of all our guests, the party felt kinda small—actually, dull—especially with everyone acting all polite and proper-like. Even Della, just when we needed some livening up. Conor cut the chocolate cake (his favorite), and I scooped vanilla ice cream. Since it was so cold out, I'd made hot chocolate, which everyone seemed to appreciate. (Alex and I put a little tipple in ours.)

When the life seemed to have fizzled out of the party, I knew it was time. I asked Conor if he'd run get more stove wood for us out in the barn. The day had turned raw, and the wood heater was eating up my stockpile on the porch. "The room's feeling a little chilly," I said, rubbing my hands over my flannel shirt sleeves for effect.

Man, if looks could kill. I knew he was thinking that it was *his* birthday, so why didn't *I* go get the wood? Or Vern? But in the end, in spite of the fact he had a lot of his mama in him, he did what I asked.

"Get your jacket. I don't want you catching cold." I was just hamming it up.

He gave me the stank eye, grabbed the leather log carrier, and hurried out in the cold. As soon as he left, I told everyone the secret that somehow Duane, Alex, and I had kept—even from Della. I'd barely finished the story when Conor ran back, his face all flushed. I could tell he was fixing to cry. Not something a 16-year-old wanted to do in front of God and everyone. Especially Crystal. He threw his arms round me, and I felt him wiping his tears on my flannel shirt so no one would notice. As if we hadn't.

He asked us all to come outside, and we grabbed our coats and hurried to the barn. Cat was sitting on the hood of the Merc, licking his paws and looking mighty pleased with himself. As if *he'd* restored that old car to its current shiny condition. To be fair, more than likely he'd kept the rats away from the upholstery, for which I was grateful.

When Duane had arrived—and sure we were all inside—he'd backed the Merc out of the barn and parked it in the grass between the house and the barn. That Mercedes hadn't looked that good in a decade. Shiny black exterior. Smooth, uncracked leather inside. What we couldn't see was its reworked engine. "Duane, you're a genius with motors and engines," I said, looking more at Conor than him.

Back in the day that car had meant the world to me, and I walked over and hugged Alex about as hard as Conor had done me. He'd given me that car, taught me how to drive in it, and I'd taken it on that long journey through the Blue Ridge Mountains of Virginia to find those con artists. And myself.

Conor and I'd been practicing driving in my truck, so he was ready to roll. But he had only his learner's permit, so Alex agreed to chaperone, just like he'd done for me. Crystal and Vern and Lyle piled in and away they went, leaving Conor's childhood behind.

Chapter 29
Abit

THANKSGIVING WAS A QUIET one with the boys away for the long weekend and Della and Alex off to Chapel Hill to spend the holiday with his friends from work. So I roasted a chicken, and Matthew brought some amazing vegetables. *Sides* he called them, a carryover from when he did professional cooking. Mollie and Red had a field day with all the scraps we just happened to drop.

When Della got back on Saturday, she invited me over for dinner. We sat round drinking beer while Alex made a fish pie with salmon and some kind of crackly stuff on top he called phyllo. Della baked gingerbread for dessert, which got even better topped with whipped cream. I always had a great time with those two. Mollie did too. She and Rascal were rassling and having fun.

I asked about the threats, and Della said they'd stopped. I could tell by the look on her face she'd had something to do with that. I nodded for her to go on.

"The last prank involved dog turds in the store mailbox. What with all the bullet holes already in it, I couldn't get it clean, and our mail carrier refused to leave mail anymore. Now I have to drive to the post office every day. When I heard about you almost getting run off the road, I'd had it. All I could think to do was place a couple of classified ads in the *Watauga Democrat* and *Blowing Rocket*. I don't remember the exact wording now, but something about the family secrets were safe, we just wanted to return something to Daisy Dawson."

"That sounds pretty tame for you," I offered.

"Well, I might have added something about their cretinous threats and fascist symbols, but I couldn't say what I really wanted to in the newspapers."

"Seems to have worked."

"So far so good. But unless we get a break soon, I'm ready for all this to be over."

That again. I was surprised, given how she'd always liked our capers even better than me. Maybe it was the lull—or end if Della had her way—in Daisy's investigation. Or how distracted she and Alex had seemed. That evening I'd caught them whispering about something, and when I asked, Della looked kinda sad when she said, "There's a time for everything, Honey."

I didn't know what she meant, but looking back, I figured I chose not to know.

WHEN WE GOT HOME, Mollie jumped outta the truck and ran off to do her business. I'd forgotten to leave any lights on, and the night swallowed her whole. I took a moment to appreciate the heavens, the stars shining bright without the moon to dull their fire.

I was humming a Bill Monroe favorite—"Blue Moon of Kentucky"—when I opened my front door and the song died in my throat. The smell of skunks was more pungent *in* the house than out. Someone musta tangled with those critters as they roamed my yard looking for their dinner.

Before the door was full open, I reached for my wood shotgun. I sure hoped whoever hid in the dark couldn't tell the difference. I raised the gun in front of me and heard him speak.

"I mean you no harm."

My heart beat loud, like a bass fiddle keeping time with my words. "And that's why you frightened me to death, waiting *inside* my home? You've already taken my most prized possession, which isn't even mine, you ..." My words caught in my throat, fear turning it dry and scratchy. I stepped closer, the gun pointed at his chest.

"Your door wasn't locked, and it's colder than a politician's heart out there. You have no need for that gun. And I have no idea what you mean about taking a prized possession. I have nothing of yours. Except answers. Violet sent me. I'm her boy, Harley. We heard about you looking into my aunt's disappearance, though why you care some sixty years later none of us can fathom."

I couldn't make sense of his words, made more confusing somehow by the dark. I held the gun on him and stepped toward the floor lamp. When I switched it on, he looked like he'd sounded—just an ordinary fellow looking for answers in a messed-up world. I nodded for him to go on.

"Daisy and Violet want me to bring you to their home."

I thought for a moment, my mind still struggling. Eventually I found my voice. "I can't go until tomorrow, and Della Kincaid has to come with me."

Chapter 30
Abit

"I THINK SOMEONE'S BEEN watching too much television," Della grumbled as Harley lowered a burlap sack over her head.

The night before, it had taken some convincing, but I finally got Harley to leave and come back the next morning so Della could join us. I assured him we wanted answers too, so we wouldn't be running off or calling the law. When he said six o'clock, I couldn't object. Didn't matter. When I called Della, she said yes without even asking—or caring—how early we'd have to go.

But now he was putting sacks over our heads and strapping us into the backseat like a coupla gangsters. Luckily, they were newish sacks that didn't stink of fertilize or rotted potatoes. I could only hope Harley had decent suspension in his SUV because we were kinda helpless in the back.

Like they did in the movies, I tried to remember what direction we turned and how long we were on which road. I gave up after half an hour. We traveled a long ways on what felt like the same road until he started taking twists and turns a bit too fast for my liking.

"Seems awfully cloak and dagger," Della whispered.

I nodded, but of course she couldn't see that. Harley hadn't said a word. Not even *shut up* the whole trip. In spite of the sacks, the trip didn't feel particularly scary. Just long and tedious.

When he finally stopped his SUV, Harley opened my door first, unbuckled and untied everything, and helped me outta the back. "Stay right there," he said, real strict-like. Then he did the same for Della. He took us each by an arm and guided us toward a handsome cabin overlooking mountains not as tall as ours. I reckoned we'd headed north to Virginia.

An older woman stood on the porch and waved at us. Like we were just a couple of visitors instead of kidnap victims. I knew there was no point in being in a snit if I wanted to get answers, but I was struggling with that. I looked over and saw Della biting her lip, trying for the same.

"Come in, and please forgive my nephew. He's very protective of me, which I do appreciate. I imagine you could use some coffee and the bathroom."

Daisy (at least that was who I figured she was) looked younger than the 77 or 78 she woulda been. She stood tall with her white hair in a chin-length cut, something I believe women called a bob. Dressed in a long black skirt with a white blousy top, she wore a string of colorful handmade beads round her neck. She looked pretty.

When we went inside, Della headed to the bathroom. The cabin was laid out a lot like my house, so naturally I knew where the kitchen was. Someone had made biscuits and the coffee smelled fresh. I tucked into both. It felt kinda strange, like going to a church potluck where you didn't know anyone but stuffing your face anyway.

When I got back from my turn in the bathroom, I refilled on both biscuits and coffee. I noticed Della was sticking to coffee. The woman motioned for us to settle in the living room. Della and I sat on the couch, while she chose the recliner opposite us. Harley kept watch by the front door.

"Harley tells me you have something for me," the woman said.

I was reaching for my satchel when Della laid her hand on my arm. "Yes, we do, but first you need to give us something. Answers. We've done a lot of work to get this far."

Harley stepped closer, but the woman motioned for him to sit back down. Like us, she knew she needed to behave to get what she wanted.

"Just who are you?" Della asked. "And how did Harley know we had something that may be yours?"

The woman ignored the first question. "I believe you placed an ad in the *Watauga Democrat*?" I looked at Harley, who was nodding.

"And did he send all those threatening notes to me at my store? Or try to run Abit off the road?" Della asked, anger making her voice quiver.

Harley and the woman exchanged looks of confusion too real to be acting. "I know nothing about threatening notes or some kind of road rage." She paused and tugged on her beads, trying to get her own anger under control. Finally, she cleared her throat and said, "Let's start over—at the beginning. You know me as Daisy, but I changed that early on to Dee. I couldn't see going through life sounding like a comic-strip character, especially when wrinkles started to show."

"We knew someone who called himself Dee because his parents had named him Dusk," I added out of nerves. It was useless information, and yet it seemed to relax Daisy a little.

"Ah, hippy parents, no doubt," she said, smiling. "Yes, I watched them come and go around here. I was just old enough to miss all that. A shame, really. Looked like fun." She paused before adding, "And I changed my last name to Underwood, the same as my Cousin Evie, the one who took me in." Daisy nodded toward my satchel. "And I believe you know why. That last night in Blowing Rock was decades ago, and yet it's never far away. I was writing in the diary when I heard someone coming. I stashed it quickly in the secret compartment of the dresser. Daddy told me to come with him, and what choice did I have?"

"And you've lived here ever since?" I asked.

"Yes. I had a good life here with Evie. I attended college in Roanoke and spent my entire career as a school teacher for the children in Grayson County. Until I retired six years ago, about the time Evie passed." She went on a while about her teaching and the children she'd loved. Funny, when she recalled her life's work, the years seemed to melt away. She looked like a woman half her age.

"But what good did it do to hide away if your daddy knew how to find you?" I asked.

"Oh, I was happy to see Daddy. I wanted *him* to come visit."

My stomach churned so bad I feared I might lose those biscuits and coffee. Daisy picked up on that quick-like.

"Oh, dear man, you have the wrong idea. It wasn't my father I was bothered by. It was my brother, Dill. My mother's favorite. She'd never listen to me when I tried to tell her what was going on."

I couldn't believe my ears. It took me a while to get my head round her news. I sipped at my coffee, but that made my stomach churn more.

"Around these parts it's not a stretch to imagine you must have had an overbearing father," Daisy said, looking kindly at me.

"More like distant."

"That can be overbearing in its own way. But don't let that color everything. Not all fathers are like that. Mine was a lovely man, and I missed him every day we were separated. I'm sure you've heard the gossip. Yes, he drank. Some. Life comes at you hard, no matter who you are. Daddy was a gentle soul. He quit drinking after he brought me here. By then he knew how much his children needed him. He always did the best he could to protect me.

"I stopped hating him—Dill—long ago. Hate is like a river that's broken its banks, eroding everything it touches. Of course that doesn't mean you just get over it. I still feel vestiges of deep sorrow. Some things never quite leave you, lingering in the shadows. But as long as you recognize they're there, they don't control you."

I felt sick thinking about all the bad assumptions I'd made. Della had warned me about that, but I'd plowed ahead and gotten things all twisted up. "Don't you want Dill punished?" I asked, clinging to the idea this whole hateful mess could be straightened out.

Daisy managed a sad smile. "As I just said, I've had a good life. I've heard rumors that Dill's hasn't gone as well."

Just then a woman came through the back door. Harley walked over and hugged her.

"This is my sister, Violet," Daisy said. "Violet, meet Abit and Della." We nodded at her, but she kinda glared back.

"We thought you were working for Dill," Violet nearabout spat at us, her eyes hard like black stones. "That's why Harley used those feed sacks. We can't have Dill coming up this way."

Della shook her head. "No way are we working for Dill. You've done such a good job of living without him, you may not realize he stopped being a threat years ago. He's in no condition to search for you or bring you any more harm."

Daisy nodded. "To be fair, he was as much a product of our strange household as any of us. Our mother was what we now call bi-polar. Untreated. That affects everyone in its path, just like alcohol." She thought for a moment before adding, "They say forgive and forget. I'm able to forgive, especially after all these years. But I can't forget. And I don't want to ever see Dill again. He's got my forgiveness. That's enough."

She offered us more coffee and biscuits, but even I'd had enough. We sat a while in merciful quiet. My head was throbbing with shame and chagrin. After a time, Daisy went on. "Violet was a victim too. She's eight years younger than me, a surprise baby, so she was only 6 when I left home. She had no idea what was going on, just that her older sister was suddenly gone and her family in shambles."

Daisy took a deep breath. "That last time was the worst. I'd had a good day at school until I got caught chewing gum. Today principals and teachers wish they had such innocent troubles to deal with, but back then it meant demerits. I had to stay after school, and in March, it got dark early. I was scared walking home, so I ran part of the way—until I got a stitch in my side and had to slow down. I limped along, and when I saw our house, I started to relax. But *he* was waiting. My new dress was ripped when I got to the house. Daddy was away on house calls, and Mother made light of it, something about not playing so rough at recess. When Daddy got home, I heard them quarreling. The next day Daddy brought me here to Tater Hill—just outside of Galax." She stopped and kinda chuckled. "Well, you already know that, don't you?"

"No ma'am, we don't know where in the world we are," I said. "Thank you for telling us." I looked over at her sister and back at her. "When did you and Violet get reunited?"

"We've been in touch for years, thanks to her determination," Daisy said, smiling at Violet. "Otherwise, I don't believe we'd have found each other again." Violet nodded, but didn't return the smile.

Daisy turned toward Della. "I may not get out much, but the Internet is a faithful companion. I looked you up, Della, or should I say, Ghoulfriend?" I couldn't believe it, but Della blushed. Not something you see every day. "You've had an impressive career."

Della nodded and motioned toward my satchel. I reached in and handed the diary to Daisy. She pulled on some reading glasses as Violet stepped behind her so she could read over her shoulder.

"I've wondered all these years about this book. I'd hoped no one had found it, especially Mother or Dill." We sat silent while they leafed through it careful-like, trying not to damage the fragile pages. Daisy smiled at some of the entries, held others up for Violet to see closer, but the last pages made them both uneasy. They closed the book. "There's time for more of that later," she said, her voice low as she set her glasses and diary on a maple table that looked handmade.

"Well, if it's any comfort, I don't believe anyone had found it before me, and only me and Della have read it. Her friend Alex knows about it, as does your cousin Wallis Harding, but he doesn't know what's in it. He just helped us look for you. Asking round to your cousins and all."

"I guess one of them sent the threats," Della said, sounding resigned to not knowing for sure.

"That's not our style," Daisy said. "But yes, there's been talk. In addition to the ad you placed, Harley was at the feed store near his home in Blowing Rock when a cousin—who will remain nameless—came up to him, complaining about your investigation into our family."

Had to be that Darlene Cunningham, but at this point, I didn't care. Bringing her up would just spoil the mood we'd finally achieved. But my lingering shame wouldn't let go. Daisy noticed.

"We all do things we're uncomfortable with, Abit, but in the end it matters more what we do about them. How we change." She let that sink in before adding, "I can tell you are special. Were you a caul baby?"

"No ma'am, not that I know of, though I heard Mama talking about when that happens. They say it's a sign of good fortune, so I'd say definitely no. Early on I wasn't quite right and that ..."

"Like I said, you *are* special," Daisy interrupted. "That's different from what you're talking about. I also see you're a musician."

"How in the ...?"

"Your callused fingers. What instrument?"

We talked a while about the mando, and then Della piped up. "He's making a mandolin. When he attended the Hickson School in Boone, he learned woodworking and has become a fine craftsman," she bragged, making me squirm.

Daisy smiled and said The Hicks was a good school. "I've referred a few students there, where they excelled. You may know one ... he's about your age."

She gave a name. I wanted to know him real bad, to have a fellow student who'd also connected with Daisy, but I'd never heard of him.

She stood and said she was feeling tired. (I knew the feeling, and I'd seen Della yawn a time or two.) Violet kinda fussed over Daisy, but she gently shrugged her off. They both walked us out to the SUV, where Harley was already sitting in the driver's seat.

"Thank you for caring what happened to me," Daisy said as she shook our hands. "You went to a lot of trouble to find me and return the diary. I don't know what I'll do with it, eventually, but at least now it's safe." She patted her nephew on the shoulder. "Harley, no need for those sacks on the way home. We know they're good people."

When we got in the backseat, I scooted past two brown paper sacks. I checked inside and saw someone had fixed us each ham biscuits, celery sticks, and an apple for the ride home. But Della and I both fell asleep before the first bite.

Chapter 31
Della

I WAS BURSTING WITH news for Abit, but he wasn't answering his phone. It'd been a week since our trip to Tater Hill, and we hadn't talked since. We'd both needed time to recover from that adventure.

Harley'd had to wake us in front of Coburn's. Neither one of us remembered the trip home, burlap sacks or not. We dragged ourselves upstairs, and I headed straight for the Rancilio. After some good strong coffee, we talked a while about Dill never having to face legal justice. We both agreed his life was a sentence more severe than any judge could deliver.

We never did find who'd sent those threats. Or tried to run Abit off the road. Likely a cousin or two who didn't like our looking into their family matters. Kinfolk could be mighty protective, even when they didn't much care for one another.

But now I had good news for Abit, though I didn't want to leave it in a voicemail. When he hadn't answered by eleven o'clock, I told Annie I'd be back when I got back. She said fine, but

I could tell my delinquent attitude was wearing thin.

I drove out to Hanging Dog, assuming Abit was in his workshop and had forgotten to turn on his phone. He did that sometimes. But not this time. His truck was gone.

He hadn't taken Mollie, so at least we got to play for a while. I'd've brought Rascal if I'd known I'd have to wait so long. Then again, this gave me a chance to bask in the specialness of this dog. All dogs are wonderful, but Mollie was at the top of the list.

She put on quite a floorshow for me, going round and round chasing that pesky white-tipped tail of hers. When she gave up ever catching it, she dragged over a well-chewed rope toy, tossing it around and pushing it into my hands to throw. We were on what felt like round one-hundred when I heard a truck coming up the drive.

Abit jumped out before the truck seemed to have fully stopped. "Della, what's wrong? My phone went on the fritz, and I had to go to Newland to get a new one." He held out the evidence, as though he were guilty of something.

"Nothing's wrong. In fact, it's very right—I found your mandolin. At least we think it's yours."

He looked stunned. Around here, good news could take more time to sink in than bad.

"One of my customers is married to a luthier, oddly or fatefully named Luther. The other morning in the store she pointed at the 'HAVE YOU SEEN THIS MANDOLIN?' poster I'd made from a photograph Alex took of you at a concert with a closeup of the mandolin. That poster had been up in the store for weeks without even a nibble, but now we have a full-blown lead."

I gave Abit the rest of the details Luther had shared with me. He wasn't absolutely certain it was Abit's, but given the details his wife had told him, he thought it likely. I did love that about the store. I may not have that many friends in Laurel Falls, not the kind you can plop down on their sofa and be yourself with, but I did know just about every interesting person in the area.

"How did Luther come by it, Della?" Abit was trying not to get excited, but newfound hope gave his voice a lift.

"He said a woman about your age brought in an exquisite old mandolin with a crack somewhere."

"What kinda crack?" Abit asked, short of breath. "Where?"

"I don't know the nomenclature, Honey, but Luther is one of the best, at least according to his wife. He invited us to come by anytime today. I'll go with you, if you want."

He nodded, mumbling something about getting his hands on the scoundrel who did this.

For a split second I thought about going to the store first to make sure everything was okay, but then I thought *nah. Annie's fine.* So we hopped in my Jeep and drove to Luther's shop.

The reunion was a success. Abit got all dreamy as he cradled his mandolin once again. The damage was in what they called the scroll. He told Luther to go ahead and make the repairs; he'd gladly pay for them.

Before we left, Luther gave us the "new owner's" address, with none of that client confidentiality you might bump against in a big city. He said Annabelle McGovern was one of those second-homers in a posh development in Beaverdam. "Acted posh too," he added.

We were both eager to talk with this Annabelle character, so I drove fast to Beaverdam. I knew where that development was—it had provoked protests from locals because it obstructed critical wildlife patterns. Of course that didn't bother the county officials who approved it, even though a viable alternative had been proposed.

Abit and I both wondered what kind of story Annabelle had swallowed when she purchased the mandolin. It needed to be a darn good one to ease my mind. Otherwise, I couldn't dismiss her culpability, at least her knowledge that the deal was shady, if not hot.

When we drove up, we could see a palatial home set at the end of the long, gravel road, a prime spot overlooking the Unaka

Mountains. Breathtaking, especially on this sunny December day. An attractive woman worked in one of the gardens, pulling out what appeared to be last year's tomato plants. She stopped and waved, as though she were expecting us.

"Hello, are you lost? I get a lot of folks out here who are." She chuckled, her voice soft and honeyed, just a hint of Southern accent. She took off her gloves to shake our hands. Very formal.

Abit seemed to have swallowed his tongue. In part because he'd never been comfortable with confrontation, but also because she was strikingly beautiful. Long sandy-colored hair in a simple plait down her back, big blue eyes, and bright natural coloring. She looked to be about Abit's age, just as Luther had mentioned.

What Abit never seemed to realize was how handsome he was. Tall, muscled from hard work, wavy red hair, and a comely face. And no, that wasn't just because he was "my boy," as Alex and I were wont to call him.

They were making goo-goo eyes at one another, so I spoke up. "I've got some bad news for you, Ms. McGovern." She snapped out of her reverie and asked how I knew her name. I ignored her. "That mandolin you bought was stolen. Hot. And it belongs to Abit Bradshaw." I brandished my hand at the object of her earlier affections.

The honey dripped right out of her voice. "I paid a fortune for that instrument—from a *reputable* dealer. If it hadn't been broken, I couldn't have afforded it. I thought I was just getting an honest good deal because of the damage."

"I'm sure you did," Abit said, finally finding his voice. I could have kicked him when he added, "I'm sorry."

"Well, I have the provenance in the house, and there's no Abit Bradshaw on it. In fact, it's linked to the Bill Monroe family. His cousin was the dealer."

That knocked some sense into Abit. He knew that had to be a fake record of ownership, and I surmised he was offended that she'd bandied about his hero's name for her own benefit.

"Not likely, ma'am," Abit said. "I mean that's about as probable as all those folks who claim they came over on the Mayflower. It would've sunk with all of them on it."

Ha! Seemed Anabelle and I had something in common—we both hated being called *ma'am*. She got all red in the face and marched toward her mini-mansion. "I'll see you in court!" she snapped as she threw her gloves and trowel to the ground.

"The devil you will, sister," I shouted after her. "Sheriff Aaron Horne will be very interested in how you came by that instrument. And Luther won't be handing it over to you, I can assure you of that. You may have all the money in the world, wealth you bring up here to flaunt in the face of hard-working people, but you won't be able to buy loyalty. That's something we've got the corner on."

I started the Jeep and backed over one of her flower beds. I apologized to the chrysanthemums.

We rode along in silence, both seething for different reasons. Abit finally said, "Della, I appreciate how you stepped in for me, but don't you think you were kinda hard on Annabelle?"

Oh, that Abit. It's what I loved about him, but sometimes it irked me. "No, I don't. She was batting her eyelashes and playing that feminine crap I can't abide. She was toying with you, Honey, and I resented that."

He nodded, not so much in agreement as to put that scene behind us. We rode to Hanging Dog without saying another word.

Chapter 32
Abit

LUTHER FIXED THE MANDO so good I couldn't see the repair, even staring at the scroll. And he only charged me for materials, no labor. Man, that was so nice of him. I told him I owed him one, and any time he needed a piece of furniture, I'd return the favor.

I still felt bad about Annabelle getting ripped off and kinda embarrassed Della had given her such a hard time. I know Annabelle got snappish, but I'd've done the same if I'd lost all that money *and* a fine instrument. I found her phone number online and called. When she picked up, I said, "I'm sorry things got so heated the other day." There was a long silence, so I added, "This is Abit Bradshaw."

"I know exactly who this is, and I don't want to talk to you. You can speak to my lawyer. Luther did tell me he'd returned the instrument to you, so I'm out hundreds of dollars."

"Yeah, and that's why I want to make you a fine piece of furniture to ease the bad news. I have a good reputation round here for my work."

"Yes, I checked up on you, after you and that shrew from the little store came out."

"Don't be too hard on Della. She looks after me and can get kinda carried away sometimes. Let's let what happens next be between just you and me."

She agreed for me to come out and discuss the piece of furniture she wanted.

WHEN I GOT TO Annabelle's home the following afternoon, she was all fancied up, though maybe that's just how rich women dress. Tight pants, silky low-cut blouse, and what looked to be a pendant that had made its way, well, out of sight. She was drinking wine and asked if I would join her.

"I prefer beer, if you have such."

"I sure do. Fresh from a brewery near Murphy. I like to support the locals." She got a HipHops Brew out of a mini fridge under her well-stocked bar and handed it to me with a colorful holiday napkin wrapped round it.

I figured she'd treat me like a workman, a no count in her eyes, but she seemed relaxed and welcoming. She was so pretty and sophisticated, I couldn't help wanting her to see my worth. We made small talk as I sipped my beer, and she poured herself more wine.

Her home was awful nice inside. All decorated for Christmas with garlands of evergreen draped up the banister and over the doorframes. A tall Christmas tree full of fancy ornaments sat to the side of a massive picture window looking out at the mountains. For some reason I felt kinda relieved I didn't see any mistletoe, even though the trees round here were eat up with the stuff.

"I love it here," she said, taking another big gulp of wine. When she asked me to join her in her bedroom, I could feel my face flush. She laughed. "Oh, Abit. You *are* adorable. I just mean to see where I need a nightstand next to my bed."

Her bedroom was nothing short of luxurious: king-size bed with lots of throw pillows and more picture windows with an eastern view promising amazing sunrises. She'd decorated for Christmas in here too. An antique Santa collection musta cost as much as my mando.

I didn't notice any pictures of a hubby on her dresser or nightstand, but you never knew. So I asked.

"Oh, he's long gone," she said, waving her hand while she drank another big slug of wine. "I got this house and he got the one in Atlanta. That view is all I need." She played peek-a-boo with the necklace chain, and even I knew she was doing that on purpose.

I sensed what a strong woman she was—she knew what she wanted and went after it. I struggled with some feelings of my own, especially since I was in her bedroom, sitting on her bed to measure the space that needed a stand. My throat felt dry in spite of the beer, but finally I managed to say, mostly outta nerves, "This is a beautiful bedroom."

"Yes it is, though I like to call it my *badroom*."

I jumped up so fast I knocked some of the throw pillows on the floor and nearly tripped over them as I tried to leave. "I have everything I need. I'll be in touch, er, I mean you'll hear from me," I blurted as I scurried toward the front door. Which was locked. I fumbled with the deadbolt and finally felt fresh air on my face. I could hear Annabelle laughing as I closed the door behind me.

On the drive home, I kept going over and over what had just happened. I'd be lying if I didn't say it felt good to have a woman show favor toward me, for whatever reason. I'd lost touch with that, what with Fiona leaving me and Annie's lack of interest.

At the same time, I kicked myself for feeling guilty about taking back the mando that was rightly mine. Annabelle had money to burn. Why did I offer to make her that blasted nightstand? I didn't know how I'd get it to her, but I did know one thing: it wasn't going to be me.

Chapter 33
Della

I KNEW I'D GONE a little overboard at Annabelle McGovern's, but I wasn't sorry. Something was off about that woman. I didn't trust her, and I found her side of the story unconvincing. *Reputable dealer* and *provenance* sounded a little highfalutin for Laurel Falls, even for a second-homer. I stewed over it, and when I couldn't let go, I drove to Newland to see Sheriff Horne.

"Why didn't you ask her who sold her the stolen mandolin?" he asked once we'd settled in with doughnuts and coffee at Cookies, the café just down from the jail. "I've never known you to shy away from accosting people."

"Oh, I accosted her all right. And we *did* ask—she said a 'reputable dealer.' But yeah, we should have pressed that, though I doubt we'd've gotten any more out of her."

"So why did you accost her?"

"For the way she was toying with Abit. Playing with his feelings. I got so mad, I had to leave before I had the opportunity to ask more about her ill-gotten gains."

"And you think *I* should." A statement, not a question.

"I do. It *is* your job, you know."

"So now you're my Chief?"

"Come on, Horne. A crime has been committed. Make that *crimes*. All these burglaries need to be solved—and stopped. I lost a flat-screen, Alex had a new car stereo ripped out of his car, and Abit had a valuable mandolin stolen."

"My deputy took your statements."

"More than two weeks ago, and nothing's happened. I can't believe you're still sitting on this. This thievery won't end here."

"For your information, Della, I haven't been sitting on things. We just haven't caught a break. Until now." He paused and added, "Thanks to you." I raised my eyebrows at him. "Once again."

I *had* brought Horne more leads than anyone in Avery County. "Okay, just go out and see Madame McGovern. She's very attractive. Who knows? She might take a shine to you, like she did Abit." I doubted that, but you never knew. Power can be a turn-on for some.

He nodded, unaware he'd dripped blueberry filling down the front of his shirt.

WHEN I CALLED HORNE a few days later, he told me Annabelle had clammed up on him, pouting about how much she'd lost. Suddenly she couldn't recall how to get in touch with Bill Monroe's so-called cousin. He assured her he was on the case and would keep her posted, which told me any shine had been all his.

Abit and I tried to do some detecting—mostly phone calls and asking around. What little we came up with we turned over to Horne. To be honest, my heart wasn't in it; I was getting tired of running into brick walls and being threatened. Not forever, just for now. With Christmas in a week or so, I was sick and tired of dwelling on the machinations of mankind.

I invited Abit to come over and help me wrap presents for the boys and make Christmas cookies for him to take home. It felt good to stand in the kitchen together, making—and eating—something we could all enjoy. I reminded myself to cherish times like these.

Chapter 34
Abit

CONOR AND VERN COULDN'T stop eating those cookies Della and I'd made, and they kept sneaking over to shake the presents she'd sent home. A few days ago we'd put up the tree—one from our property that looked fine outside but kinda straggly oncet it came inside. Like every year. And like every year, it turned festive oncet we'd trimmed it with family decorations and new ones Vern had fashioned from my wood scraps.

It was shaping up to be a nice Christmas. The boys were already off from school, I'd mostly finished my new mando, and Fiona's was all polished and ready for Conor to take to Asheville in a few days. Then they'd be going back the day after Christmas, what Fiona called Boxing Day, so Bryce could take them all skiing. (And no, I would never refer to him as their *step-father*!) I hoped they'd come home in one piece.

I dreaded how lonely the farm would seem without our everyday ways—simple things like sharing what they'd had for dinner at school or watching them play their games with a fierce seriousness. Sure, at first glance those matters seemed ordinary, easy to take for granted, but they were precious.

The best Christmas gift came early. Ever since Tater Hill, I'd been pondering how stuck I'd been on the idea that Daisy's daddy had to be the one causing her harm. The truth of that situation—and what it said about me—brought me up short. I'd had that happen before, when I'd grow sick and tired of my own complaints voiced over and over, but this ran deeper yet. I'd let old anger color my thinking and lead me down the wrong path. Our time with Daisy had helped me see things in a new way, especially with Daddy and how our lives together had played out. I'd need to work on all that more, but already it had given my heart ease.

Mollie and I headed out to the shop to finish up that stupid nightstand for Annabelle and a couple of other orders I'd promised before Christmas. While I was working on a bookshelf, the crows started making an awful racket. They always seemed so irritated with their lot in life, I found myself wishing they were the ones that flew south each winter instead of their sweet-singing cousins.

All I could figure was Sparky or Cat were bothering something the crows considered theirs (which pretty much summed up most of the troubles in the world). I grabbed my jacket and stepped outside to see what was going on. I could hear a vehicle coming up the drive—probably UPS—and headed its way to collect my package. Only it wasn't Big Brown, but rather a newish red pickup I didn't recognize.

I nearly dropped my teeth when Shiloh hopped outta the truck and ran past me toward the woodshop without even a howdy-do. No jacket, just wearing his Zen togs—baggy pants, loose shirt, beads, and of course patchouli. I could hear Sparky chattering up in the tree, but surely that was just a coincidence.

"It's all your fault, Abit. I never should have stopped off here," he said oncet we were inside the shop, warming ourselves by the woodstove.

"What kinda hogwash is that from Mister Mindfulness?"

"I know, I know. Not really your fault. It's just that when I came here earlier, I felt like, well, *me* again. I tried to get back into the swing of things in D.C., but I struggled. Then a miracle happened. Well, of sorts. Charlene's old man got caught in an illegal trading scheme. He pled out and will be going to one of those country-club prisons in upstate New York. Charlene is making plans to move nearby. Fortunately I'd saved enough to buy the truck and keep myself clothed and fed for a while." He looked over at the empty guestroom I'd built next to my woodshop. "Any chance I could rent that again? Work here?"

Funny what time and circumstance can do when they team up. Early on, I was often glad to see the back of him, but now his wishes were just what I'd been hoping for. (Though to be honest, Shiloh hadn't come to mind when I'd prayed for help.)

When I reached my hand out, trying to remember one of Shiloh's fancy handshakes, he gave me a big bear hug. I followed suit and sighed with a mix of happiness and relief. I laughed out loud when he mumbled, "I think of us as companion animals."

Not long after, it dawned on me that Shiloh could deliver the nightstand to Annabelle. I wished I could've been a fly on the wall for that. I didn't tell him anything about her, just that he needed to take it to her bedroom. He came home looking a little shook up. I didn't ask.

Chapter 35
Abit

I FINALLY FINISHED THE mando. Turned out beautiful, the flame in the grain lighting up the wood in perfect harmony with the instrument's gentle curves. It even felt good in my arms.

But it sounded worse than a washboard bass.

Della stopped by with more presents for the boys, and I showed it to her. She too admired its fine appearance. When I told her it sounded terrible, she didn't believe me. Until I played "Liberty," one of her favorites. It's a merry little tune—only not that time.

"Do you think it just needs fine-tuning?" she asked, trying to be polite.

"I'm a woodworker, not an instrument maker. Like you said all along." To her credit, she never said *told you so*. "I've decided to mount it on the living room wall as a piece of art. It's pretty on the outside even though inside it never found its music."

"That sounds like something Shiloh would've said at one of his seminars," Della said. She and Shiloh had never been close, but when she'd pulled up, she did give him what appeared to be a genuine hug.

I still worried what I'd do for a mando when the Rollin' Ramblers performed again after the holidays, but I left that for another day.

I put the kettle on, and we sat round drinking tea and finishing the cookies we'd made together. It felt like old times. Della told me about her first Christmas living on her own in D.C. "It was lonely in a way, but at least no one was getting drunk and ruining the day." Her alcoholic parents had died a few months before in a car wreck. "I went alone to a restaurant in D.C. owned by Muslims. That way I didn't feel guilty about making them work on Christmas Day. I'd never had Middle Eastern food before, and the dishes—tabouleh, baba ghanoush, kofta, baklava—were divine. They've stayed favorites ever since."

When she asked me about my favorite Christmas, I didn't hesitate. "That would be Vern's first Christmas with us, when he was just 8 year old. Times were lean, especially after those murder-ballad murders had pulled me away from my woodshop, and Fiona had to send money to her father. I know you recall from our wedding that he was an alcoholic, and that summer he'd been sick and couldn't hold down a job.

"I was determined we'd have a good Christmas. Fiona and I'd picked up a few things for the boys, but not as much as we'd've liked.

So we coaxed twenty dollars from the piggy bank we threw odd bits of change into all year and headed to Newland on Christmas Eve. At the five-and-dime, we each went our own way with five dollar in our pockets. Somehow we had to find gifts for one another with just that much. I recall Vern bought me a small box of hankies with violets printed on the edges and smelling of lavender. I didn't want to hurt the boy's feelings, but I got the giggles. I told him I loved them—and him—but they were ladies' hankies. He looked pitiful as he explained they were cheaper than the men's handkerchiefs. I laughed so hard I needed to use one of the hankies, and that made us all laugh. Conor got me an apothecary jar of M&Ms that looked so festive with all those colors, like little ornaments inside. I remember buying a pretty ribbon for Fiona's hair and a big bone for Mollie. I wish I could remember all the other gifts, but they've slipped away with the years."

I shook my head, surprised by all the memories that came pouring back. I'd come to find that often happened on the cusp of big change.

Chapter 36
Abit

THE PHONE RANG JUST after Della left, while I was clearing dishes.

"You need to get over here, Abit." Wallis.

"Right this minute? Are you kidding round?"

"I'm serious as church," he said and hung up.

I knew better than to ignore him. He wouldn't bother unless it were important. Thirty minute later I pulled into his drive. He stuck his head outta his front door and motioned for me to come in.

I wasn't sure at first what I was looking at. The living room ceiling had a web of twisted ropes with two cast iron frying pans suspended from them and trip wires all round the baseboard. Like something Rube Goldberg would've made.

"What in the world?"

"I caught that guy who was stealing stuff, like your mando and Kincaid's TV."

"How? Where is he?"

"Oh, that SON OF A GOAT is in the Newland jail. Sheriff Horne came and got him. I just wanted you to see this before I took it all down."

He went over to the stove and poured me a cup of strong coffee. It tasted fresh. I motioned for him to go on.

"Well, I got this idea, and I set this contraption up to catch him. And it worked."

"How'd you figure he'd come here next?"

"I got this notion about what a coincidence it was that you, Alex, and Della all had stuff stolen. I hadn't heard about anyone else getting burgled, and I've got a pretty good pipeline. Doesn't that pinpoint something for you?"

"That we're all friends?"

"Well, yes, that is true. But how about that we'd all had dinner together a while back at Adam's Rib? I got to recalling how our conversation went that day, what with you crying about having to return that valuable mandolin come Christmas, and Alex kinda bragging about a new stereo in his already outrageous German tank. He even mentioned Della's flat screen TV. And what have the three of you reported stolen?" He did that thing people do, tapping the side of their head to say they're smart.

And of course he was. But what really grabbed me was how Wallis's voice had taken on a different tone, both now and earlier on the telephone. I had trouble believing it, but yes, I'd say it was *respectful*. Gone was the ornery edge that had colored so many of his comments over the years. Thinking back, he and I'd worked a near-miracle together almost exactly six year ago, but even finding that killer against all odds hadn't gained his full respect. Why now? Because it involved kinfolk? Or because I was older? Whatever, something had changed. Not to mention he hadn't called me *young Abit* today. He'd used just my name, sorry as it was.

"Pretty clever, Wallis, but I don't recall you bragging or saying anything about fine belongings."

"I didn't, Abit. Not until I went back a coupla nights ago when Keaton was in town. I made a point of sitting in that waiter's area and went on and on about my fiddle. You'da thought it were a Stradivarius. I came home and put the fiddle on display—right here." He pointed to an area in line with the back window where the complicated ropes and wires were set in a way the burglar wouldn't notice until he was tangled in them. "And I left the window unlocked. I waited, then fell asleep, but he woke me with all his hollerin'."

I started laughing when Wallis did his best to re-enact that scene. "How'd you hold him 'til Airhorn arrived?"

"He was tangled in the ropes and knocked silly by that fry pan, so it was easy."

Like that cast iron skillet hitting the burglar's head, I was suddenly struck by the notion that Wallis had solved this mystery for *me*. Della had already found my mando, but Wallis took it even further to put my mind at rest about who'd stolen my most precious possession. I felt deep gratitude he'd caught the culprit and told him so.

He just shrugged. "Airhorn even found Della's flatscreen in the guy's house, but Alex's stereo was long gone."

We visited a while after that, me telling him how much I appreciated his help with finding Daisy. He nodded and said he'd enjoyed himself—except for his time in jail. We made promises to stay in touch, and I hoped it wasn't just the kind of thing people say to make parting easier.

As I started to leave, I stopped in my tracks. "Wait a minute. How'd you call Horne and me to come over?"

He held up a cellphone. "Keaton. Early Christmas present."

Chapter 37
Abit

CHRISTMAS MORNING WE WERE all together, eating flapjacks I'd made, the boys drinking milky coffee while I sipped my stronger brew. Kinda calm for a Christmas morning with two young'uns, but they were getting older and had already opened their gifts.

The only thing missing, we realized oncet we'd broken out of our maple-syrup stupor, was Mollie. No Christmas floorshow, no shenanigans, no playing with her new ropey toy.

"Who let her out?" I asked.

"You did, Daddy," the boys said in a chorus of two. A little sadness was already creeping into the tenor of their voices.

Mollie never went out for long, unless we were with her. And by our best account, it had been almost an hour since we'd last seen her. In all the hubbub of the morning, we'd lost track.

I went to the door and called out for her. She hadn't heard me do that often—she was usually by my side. But still, she'd know what I wanted.

Only she didn't come.

Well, let me tell you, that put a damper on things. We sat quiet-like, best we could. Eventually, though, we remembered why we were celebrating this day and thought about that for a good while. Then, even though it was His birthday and all, I couldn't stop myself from asking a favor—to help Mollie return to us safe and sound.

After a time, I noticed something special outside and called the boys to the front porch. I regretted my excited tone the minute they ran into the room, big grins on their faces. That changed quick-like when they realized I wasn't calling them to greet Mollie.

But snow on Christmas, even here in the mountains, is a wonderful thing. Sure, we saw our share of the white stuff, but it seemed to fall only when you needed to drive somewhere important—not often on Christmas Day. We stood on the porch as long as we could, watching a gentle whiteness settle over the landscape. When the cold pinched our faces and behinds too hard, we scurried inside and I reluctantly closed the door. I couldn't imagine what was keeping that dog.

I tended the fire and started thinking about Christmas dinner. Shiloh and Matthew were joining us, and I needed to get the turkey in the oven. While I was washing some beans, I heard a scratch at the front door. It was faint, but those boys heard it too, way up in their room where they were playing a new game.

Then another scratch. By the time I got to the door, the boys were right behind me.

When I opened the door, Mollie sat there still-like, snowflakes topping each hair in her grey-and-white plume. Then the sun broke through the clouds, backlighting her in a way that—and I swear I'm not exaggerating—made it appear she had a halo.

She had a funny look on her face. As I reached down to make sure she was okay, she dropped a whopping big biscuit in my hand. Not a partially eaten one, but a whole biscuit I knew our neighbor, Jancie, had given her.

I later learned Mollie had been making the rounds that morning. Fortunately we lived on a quiet road, and she could trot safely from house to house, getting treats and ear rubs from all. I mean who could resist a face like hers?

Oncet I realized how many neighbors she'd visited, I understood it wasn't so amazing that she'd brought that biscuit home whole. She was full! But still, I've known dogs to eat themselves sick, so I held onto the notion of that biscuit being the Christmas blessing it was.

AFTER OUR BIG DINNER—ROAST turkey, cornbread dressing, cranberry relish, green beans, pumpkin pie (from Matthew—not Coburn's)—Conor came over carrying something big in a pillowslip with a bow tied round it.

"Whatcha got there, boy?" I asked.

"Something from me and Vern. For you."

They'd already given me some gifts—*men's* handkerchiefs this year and some fine wool socks—so I couldn't imagine what this was all about. When I undid the ribbon and looked inside, I nearabout dropped it.

Fiona's mandolin.

"Conor, you were meant to return this to your mama last week." I sounded kinda stern, but I was confused. And a little nervous.

"I *did* give it to her, Daddy, and I was so happy when she handed it back to me. 'Oh,' I said, 'are you letting Daddy keep it?' She patted it and told me, 'No, darling, I'm giving it to *you*—to keep it in the family.'" Conor looked up at me, his eyes wide. "And I want you to have it."

I couldn't speak for the longest time. I finally managed, "I'll think of it as a loan."

"No, Daddy. It's yours. You *are* family. *My* family." He put his arm round Vern. "*Our* family. You've given it life now for over fifteen years. It's got your music in it. Someday, when your fingers grow tired, *then* you can give it to me."

I held it, cradled it, like I'd done for so many year. It felt good in my arms, and I would love hearing its notes again. But not near as much as the music of Conor's words.

Chapter 38
Della

I MADE PLANS TO celebrate the new year with all my friends. For much of my life that would have been a very small party. Later on, when I moved to Laurel Falls, I could never have imagined how many disparate people would eventually come to mean so much to me.

Annie and I figured out how to move shelving around in Coburn's to open a good-size space for a New Year's Eve party. That evening as guests arrived, I told everyone we'd keep it simple—they could open any wine, beer, or soft drinks and raid the cheese counter, unwrap boxes of crackers, and sample whatever they'd ever wanted to try at Coburn's.

"You're not just pawning off expired meats and cheeses on us are you?" someone joked from the back. I'd put my money on Sheriff Horne.

Abit had come early to help, and he and Annie seemed more relaxed around each other. I was counting on that.

In addition to Abit, Annie, and Horne, the guest list included Annie's father, Elbert—her mother never seemed to venture beyond grocery shopping at the SuperMart out on the highway—and several other regulars. Wallis Harding came, and after he got my TV back, I told him he was a guest of honor. I could tell he still didn't know what to make of me, but he smiled.

The evening turned out more fun than I'd hoped. Annie contributed a small sound system and played a nice assortment of music—something for everyone somewhere in the mix. (She played my favorite—Marvin Gaye's "What's Going On"—several times to please me.) About eleven o'clock, Abit came over, his jaw literally dropping open as he pointed to the latest arrival: Blanche Scoggins dolled up in a sequiny black top and leather pants. I chuckled and said, "You ain't seen nothing yet!"

We lucked out that the weather had turned unseasonably warm. All the snow had melted, and the meadow hinted at a green that would thrive come spring. Some partygoers went outside to gaze at the full moon. Mollie and Rascal were already out there, chasing each other and taking advantage of all the additional hands to push their heads into for ear rubs.

Everyone returned to the store for the countdown. Midnight came and went, and we did all the routine hugging and toasting. Until the front door flew open and a dark specter entered unannounced. Father Max, dressed in his black cleric's garb. The Episcopal priest had left the area a while ago, but I'd tracked him down in Asheville. No one else would do for the ceremony.

Alex and I were getting married again.

I'd asked Annie (the only other person who knew about the wedding) to be my maid of honor. No question that Abit would be Alex's best man. After we said *I do*, Annie wheeled in a wedding cake she'd made, decorated with sprigs of mistletoe and holly berries that made it perfect.

While we were eating cake—German chocolate, my favorite—Wallis came over to where I was standing with Abit and Annie. A bit tipsy, he put his arm around Annie and slurred, "What I want to know is when you and Abit will tie the knot. Everybody knows you're keen on one another."

Abit nearly choked on his beer, and Annie looked alarmed. Wallis didn't pick up on his faux pas, making things worse when he asked Annie, "You blushing or did you rouge up?" When even the tips of her ears turned scarlet, he got his answer.

We finally cleared the place out by one o'clock. I dreaded the cleanup, but it would be a lot worse if we put it off until the next day, so I started puttering around. Alex helped.

"Della, Annie said she'd help me with this," Abit said. "Consider it my wedding gift to you, since you sprung this on me and I came without a present. Go on upstairs and start your honeymoon."

No need to ask twice. Alex and I took the steps to our home. For now.

Chapter 39
Abit

Winter 2013

AFTER THE HOLIDAYS WOUND down and the boys were in school again, I finally made it back to Coburn's. I could see Annie inside the store, but I slipped past quick-like up the stairs to Della's apartment. I wasn't quite ready to see Annie again after what happened at midnight on New Year's Eve. She gave me a kiss—and then turned and gave her daddy the same kinda kiss. Seemed I'd always be just a family friend to her.

Upstairs, Della gave me a longer than usual hug. When I looked round her apartment, I thought it seemed awful tidy. "Doing spring cleaning early?" I asked.

"Oh, I got rid of some of the tchotchkes and trinkets that accumulate after almost thirty years."

"You're not going anywhere, are you?"

"Oh, Honey, this apartment is mine for the duration," she said, busying herself in the kitchen.

Funny wording, but at the time I figured that was just Della's fancy way with words.

She made me a latte, and we swapped stories about the holidays for a while. When we'd run outta that kind of stuff, I stood and went to the door. I'd left a big box out on the stoop; I grabbed it and held it out to her. "Sorry I didn't wrap it, but it's awful big. I made you a wedding gift."

I'd taped the box pretty good so she couldn't just tear into it. She laughed at that and got a knife. When she finally got the box open, she pulled the gift outta the box and set it on her lap. Her face got all pinched.

"Hey, Della, it didn't take that long to make, and I loved working on it."

"Oh, it's not that, Honey. I love it too. Thank you." She kinda hugged it, best she could.

I'd made her a mailbox that looked just like Coburn's. She'd had to throw away her old one after all the dog turds. I sure hoped the joy riders wouldn't put bullet holes in this one.

She turned it this way and that, and I have to admit the detail was pretty good. She kept looking at it from every angle, studying it. "Oh, and that's *you*—in your chair!" That was when she started to cry. "Alex," Della called out. "Come in here, please. We need to talk with Abit."

I hadn't realized Alex was there, but he came in looking smart in a suit and tie. He gave me a big hug. My throat felt dry. I knew what bad news looked like.

"Kinda dressed up for Laurel Falls, aren't you?" I asked, trying for a joke.

"Yeah, I suppose so." He sounded nervous. Not at all like him. "Actually, I'm heading up to D.C. for a meeting."

And that's when it hit me. I'd never been in an earthquake, but I reckoned I now knew the feeling. In the blink of an eye, I couldn't get purchase on anything. The floor. The couch. The walls. Everything was helter-skelter. Della came over and sat next to me.

"We kept putting off telling you," she said, holding my hand and patting my back. After a while she went on. "I need to do something different with my life. I'm bored with the store and I've walked every trail in the woods a thousand times. In the spring, sometime in April, we're moving to our home in D.C. Alex has been renting it out, and the lease is up then."

All I heard was she was bored, and that musta included me. I felt sick.

"Abit," Alex said, "we're having trouble finding the right words. What Della said is true, but we're not bored with *you*. I can imagine it sounded that way, but you're the only reason we've stayed this long."

I wanted to go over and smash that blasted mailbox, throw it out their big window over the kitchen sink. I stood up as though I were about to do that, but Della was still holding my hand and wouldn't let go. Like she could read my mind.

"I'm deeding the store to you, Abit. I was going to leave you the store someday anyway, so why not now? The only stipulation is the apartment remains mine throughout my lifetime, so I have a place to stay when I come back to visit. Which will be often, I promise you. You know how much I used to go up to D.C. to visit Alex before he moved here? Well, I'll be coming back to Laurel Falls even more. I bet we'll even get embroiled in some capers."

I was having trouble taking all this in. I now owned the store? What in the world was I gonna do with it?

"I know this is a lot to dump on you, Abit, but I might as well finish. The only other stipulation is that Annie continues to run Coburn's, at least as long as she wants. She's doing a fine job, and for the past few months, I've been giving her more responsibility and guidance. I think she'll be pleased. I was even thinking about buying your old house to make this a whole package, but I couldn't saddle you with all those memories."

"So when were you going to tell me about this? When the truck was loaded, ready to head outta here?"

"No, no. We were just waiting for the right time. And of course there isn't one."

After that I heard her and Alex saying something about how much the boys would love visiting D.C. They had plenty of room; we could come anytime we wanted. Alex even handed me three Amtrak tickets, round trip, open dated.

But it was all a blur. I stood, made my way to the door, and fled down the stairs.

Chapter 40
Abit

ON THE DRIVE HOME, I struggled to keep my mind on the road. All I wanted to do was get to the house where I could rail and rant and throw things. But oncet there, I just lay on the bed and stared at the ceiling, where cobwebs playfully dangled, mocking me.

I couldn't imagine life without Della. Nothing before her coming to Laurel Falls held any meaning for me. My life went on just fine after Mama and Daddy passed. They'd never really been part of my life. My *real* life, the one inside. They'd fed me and clothed me, and I suppose did the best they could to keep me alive. Then Della arrived to give my life purpose. Before, everything was just black and white. Della brought color. Now I feared a return to the dullness of gray.

Finally, the dam broke. I cried until my head ached and my eyes itched. Everything felt as though it had come unwrapped.

I stayed like that for the longest time, Mollie by my side. I petted her fur until she got antsy and left me. The sun was getting low, and I knew the boys would be coming home soon, Conor driving that Merc like I used to. That made me smile.

I'd always known someday Della would leave me, but I figured it was decades away, when she finally ran outta the steam that kept her so alive. Now she'd be gone for all the days we would've had left together. I lay with that pain for a long time.

Chapter 41
Abit

IT TOOK A FEW weeks 'til I got back to my woodshop. It felt so cold and lonely this time of year, dark more often than light. So many of the birds had left, and Sparky was doing his half-hearted hibernation, making the scene only on the warmest of winter days, which this year were few. At least Cat still came round and purred.

Now that I had my old mando back, I spent more time with my music. When I'd prayed for its safe return, I'd promised I'd never take it for granted. I'd been true to my word, so far.

And I started writing songs again. "Trouble Is My Shadow" was shaping up nicely, and I'd been working on some other tunes that came to me in a dream. I'd quit writing when I'd been mired in so much misery. Sure, sorrow was what fired up Bill Monroe and other greats, but I found myself well beyond that level of sadness. You can be eat up with too much heartache to make good sense.

I'd also worked up a song for Annie: "Coming Home to You," in part because she lived in my old house, but mostly because I finally had hope about us. Not long after New Year's, she'd explained why she'd been standoffish: she could see I was still tormenting myself about Fiona. I started to object, but then I reckoned she was right.

Chapter 42
Abit

I FINALLY GOT A grip. It took a fair amount of prayer and a dose of good sense to realize Alex and Della weren't moving 'til spring, and it didn't make sense to mope round 'til then. I planned to make every day count.

At first Della seemed surprised I volunteered to give her a hand getting the store in shape before they left, but then she figured it out. I *needed* to help, like I'd done with Daisy. In the end, Daisy didn't really need my help, but I was able to relieve her mind about the whereabouts of her diary. But that wasn't so much the point. I did what *I* had to do. Same with helping Della, only more so.

I spent as much time at Coburn's as I could. It felt like the old days, except this time I was *inside* the store. And I actually felt happy most days. We cleaned every shelf, cupboard, and case, including the backrooms, where we found stuff so outta date we had to laugh. And old notices and posters, some of them connected to our capers.

Then one day in late March, when April was on the tip of our tongues, something dark swept over me. I felt sick to my stomach and couldn't think straight. I excused myself and went outside for fresh air, kicking gravel round as I paced and pondered. A pair of mourning doves echoed my sorrow.

Della would be gone in a matter of days. Sure, sometimes here in Laurel Falls, a few weeks went by when we wouldn't see each other. But it was that feeling that I *couldn't* see her that got my insides all torn up. I knew she'd be true to her word and come for visits. And I would be headed to D.C., where I'd had a blast those times I'd visited. I knew the boys would love all those museums too. That city was steeped in beauty, the manmade kind that, in its own way, rivaled the glory of nature.

But it wouldn't be the same.

I looked over at the house where I'd grown up. The steps were still mossy and, this time of year, treacherous. I reckoned life was a lot like them, one thing leading to the othern, in a pattern of sorts. We may not know it at the time, but looking back it's easy to see how we are always climbing toward home. Things that seem terrible, oncet time works off the rough edges, end up leading somewhere better, building on what came before. Like when I got yanked outta school and ended up at The Hicks. Or when we hunted that heinous ballad killer and rescued precious Vern along the way.

And when I met Della, my mother of choice.

At that moment, the thought of Della not being just down the road weighed so heavy on my heart, I didn't know how it kept beating. And yet I supposed that was just another stairstep, one I had no choice but to take. All I could do was hope someday it would lead somewhere good.

I wiped my eyes and told myself to stop all this thinking about a past I couldn't change and a future I had no idea about. When I heard tapping on Coburn's plate glass window, I looked up and saw both Annie and Della standing there, smiling. Waving at me to come back in.

I headed toward the store. On the way back, I noticed the groove I'd worn in the side of the building all those year ago as I leaned my chair against the store. It'd been painted over a number of times, but it was still there. I'd made my mark.

I opened the door and stepped inside, vowing to live my life facing forward, as the person I wished I'd been all along.

**Read an excerpt from the next book
in the series, *After Dusk*, following the
Acknowledgements and note from the author.**

YOUR FREE BOOK IS WAITING FOR YOU

VISIT
https://BookHip.com/CGPGFA
FOR YOUR FREE COPY

OR CLICK HERE TO GET YOUR FREE COPY

Acknowledgments

When I started the series with *A Life for a Life*, I honestly thought it was a one-off. But Abit kept talking with me, and before I knew it, I'd worked my way through to *Unwrapped*, the *eighth* book (including the prequel, *Waiting for You*).

Of course it wasn't just Abit that spurred me on. So did my readers, especially the ones who left uplifting reviews or wrote me such nice notes. Some shared their own mountain experiences, which often brought back even more memories for me. Thank you to each and every one of you.

For this book, I want to thank the Mandolin Café for sharing instructions for building mandolins and the heartaches that sometimes got in the way. It was a great resource for me and Abit as he built his. (And it's no reflection on them that his ended up sounding like a washboard bass!)

Thanks, too, to Gina Willis for sharing her beautiful thoughts about mandolins, Bill Monroe, and his music. And for serving as my editor and friend through all eight books. Let's do another one!

Dear Readers ...

I hope you enjoyed this book in my Appalachian Mountain Mysteries series. I sure enjoy writing them! I've been a professional writer for several decades now (I got my start in the mountains of N.C.), and it still thrills me when readers write to me. Sometimes they have questions about the stories and the characters. Other times they leave reviews and, well, make my day!

"Reminds me of *To Kill a Mockingbird* ... finding your books is like finding a rare jewel." ~J.M. Grayson

"After reading the first book, I read all the others as quickly as possible!" ~ Ruth H.

I'd really appreciate it if you'd take a minute to leave a review. (It's easy—just a sentence or two is enough.) Reader reviews are the lifeblood of any author's career. In today's online world, they can make a huge difference—so thanks in advance.

These days, I spend my time writing my Appalachian Mountain Mysteries series. I started them as a way to share amazing stories from my back-to-the-land experience in the N.C. mountains. I made mistakes by the wheelbarrow load, but I wouldn't take anything for those years.

I get a kick out of hearing from readers, so don't be a stranger! I'd love to hear your thoughts about Abit Bradshaw, Della Kincaid, and the whole Laurel Falls gang. Write me at lyndabooks@pm.me .

Happy reading!
Lynda McDaniel

P.S. I thought you might enjoy an excerpt from the next book in the series after the Book Club Discussion Guide.

P.P.S. And I hope you'll take advantage of my offer for a free subscription to **Spellbound Mystery Magazine**. Weekly issues are packed with fun facts and book recommendations that make finding a good book easy! Learn more at https://spellboundmysterywriters.substack.com/

Excerpt Book 8
After Dusk

Spruce Lake
Gragg, N.C.
June, 2015
Prologue: Erik

I dreaded the swelter awaiting me in my cabin, but I'd grown tired of the banal chatter and mindless drinking at The Way Out bar. Lately, people at work had complained that my countenance was best described as dyspeptic. (If they only knew how true that was!) I thought an early night might help.

Once home, I dragged my lounge chair on the deck into the shade of a giant oak. The webbing groaned under my weight, but the cold Pabst went down easy.

I tried to relax, but who was I kidding? That hadn't happened in years. Ten months ago when I'd moved to Spruce Lake, I had hopes of a new beginning. Then fate intervened and drew *him* into my path, igniting the wrath that had smoldered for decades.

He hadn't recognized me as we passed each other on the street, even though he had taken everything from me—wife, daughter, respect, even the nature of my breath. In a flash, the bitter tang of hate filled my mouth.

It was time to finally settle the score.

Lost in cruel memories, I was brought back to the deck by a buzzing sound. I searched for its source and was delighted to discover a wasp struggling in a large web under the eaves. Some people here call them waspers, but that made them sound cartoonish. I knew all too well they were deadly.

I studied its attempts to escape, but there was no way out. As I sipped my beer, a black spider emerged from the shadows like a gladiator.

I toasted the spider with my last sip, knowing what I needed to do.

Laurel Falls, N.C.
Summer, 2015
Chapter 1: Abit

I was sweating. Not just from the hot June day but because some guy was giving me the stank eye. His face, cool and unbothered by the heat, said he was still on the young side, maybe late twenties, but his eyes looked weary. I got one of my shivers when I saw a couple of prison tats on his neck. Blue crosses, one on each side.

I was standing in the produce department at the SuperMart, the grocery out on the highway past Laurel Falls. I didn't shop there much. The growing season had been good so far, and I got most of what I ate outta my garden or picked up at the farmers market at Coburn's General Store. Now that Annie Totherow ran the store, she'd come up with new ideas to bring in more business. It felt good to see that parking lot hopping with trucks and transactions. When I was growing up and Daddy was doing his best to run Coburn's into the ground, only a car now and again stirred up dust.

I put a bunch of grapes in my basket and cut my eyes over to where that fellow had been. Good. He was gone.

Until he wasn't.

After I picked out a few more things and went through the checkout, I caught a glimpse of someone moving up on me. I turned, ready for him, staring back hard.

"You're Mr. Bradshaw, aren't you?" he asked. "Adam, isn't it?"

"Who wants to know? And it's Abit, not Adam."

"That's right!" he said, snapping his fingers and breaking out with a big grin that made him look less scary. "We have that in common—unusual first names. They sure can be a pain in the backside."

"That right?"

"Right." He looked round, nervous-like. "You may not remember me, but I'm Dusk Holt. You and the woman from the general store, Ms. Kincaid, helped look into my family's mess." He smiled even though those memories had to be painful.

Dusk Holt. Grown up, as tall as my six-foot-three frame with muscles he'd likely worked on in prison. Blond hair flopped over his forehead and almost covering his eyes, looking more like a surfer dude than an ex-con. Except for those tats. "You were such a young'un then," I said. "I'm surprised you remember much."

"Well, my sister, Astrid, never forgot that summer, and she kept telling me all about it. And how could a kid forget that his mother had been killed?"

That hung so heavy I couldn't think of a thing to say. I knew the real story about his mother, but I'd never tell him. Not even if he asked. "Anyway, I've been trying to find Ms. Kincaid," he went on, looking round as if she were hiding behind the bread display. "Astrid told me to stop by the store, you know, and say hi and thank you." Then he bowed toward me, like he was tipping a cap. "And to you too. She said you were real nice to her, especially that day on the bus."

I was going along with this happy reunion until something struck me as odd. "How'd you recognize me? It's been what? Twenty year?"

He held up his cellphone. "Astrid again. She sent me photos of each of you. You and Ms. Kincaid."

I felt ashamed of myself, so quick to judge him. I recalled what a nice boy he'd been back then. And what dark days that family had gone through. As much as Mama had driven me crazy at times, I woulda missed her if she'd left. I was lost in those thoughts when I heard Dusk clear his throat. I jerked my attention back. "Oh, Ms. Kincaid, er, Della, moved back to Washington, D.C., leaving me Coburn's." He looked at my sack of groceries from the SuperMart and raised his eyebrows. "Oh, well, Coburn's doesn't carry everything," I said, as if I owned him an explanation. "What brings you back to town?"

"How do you know I've been gone?"

"Well, besides never seeing you in such a small place, I, er ..." I realized too late I was running my fingers along my neck.

He pulled up his collar. "That was a big misunderstanding," was all he said.

"Okay, but why'd you give me the stank eye?"

He surprised me when he laughed. "I need glasses. I was squinting to make you out. I wasn't sure if it was you, until you turned my way."

After that we stood there a while, both uneasy about what to do next. I could tell Dusk wanted to ask something, and I wanted to know why he was going by that name when as early as six year old he'd asked to be called Dee. But I reckoned we all changed over time, especially after a stay in prison.

"Well, I guess I'll be moving on. Good to see you again," I said. Not very original, but it got the job done.

"Yeah, and I'll see you better next time."

Next time? I thought, with no hint of kindness.

Dusk misunderstood my quizzical look. He put his hand up, as though he were lifting something to his face. "Yeah, when I've got my new glasses." He laughed again, like that was hilarious.

I waved behind me on the way out the door.

I drove out of the parking lot, pulled over, and called Della. We'd stayed in close touch since she'd moved a few year ago. She'd been back to visit five or six times, and the boys and I had gone to D.C. twicet before they'd each graduated from high school and left Laurel Falls behind.

"Della, you're not gonna believe who I ran into at the SuperMart."

"What are you going out there for?"

Not her too. "Grapes. And sweet corn. I didn't plant any this year, and no one at the farmer's market had any yet."

"So who was this mysterious person?"

"Dusk Holt. You know, Dee."

She was silent for a while. I knew both those kids still played on her mind. After a time, she asked, "What ever happened to him?"

"Well, it wasn't exactly old home week. Apparently he's had a rough time of it. Say, did you know Astrid now lives in Paris? And I don't mean Kentucky."

"Yeah, she sends me Christmas cards and the occasional email. She always did say she was going to get out of that place. But what did you mean by rough time for Dee?"

I filled her in on the prison tats. I heard her sigh. "How did you recognize him?"

"I didn't. He was giving me the stank eye and eventually introduced himself."

"Why?"

"Why did he introduce himself?"

"No, why was he giving you a dirty look?"

"Turned out he was just squinting at me. Said he needed glasses."

Della laughed. I guessed it was funny, oncet I thought about it. "What did he want?" she asked.

"I'm not sure, but I could tell he was after something."

"Let's hope it goes better than the first time we met him."

Chapter 2: Abit

Someone was knocking on my front door. That just about never happened. I either knew them and they walked right in, or they didn't come at all. I spent a lot of time by myself, what with my boy, Conor, traveling with a bluegrass band outta Nashville and my other boy, Vern, down in Asheville at cooking school.

Mollie wasn't used to the kind of visitors who knocked. She started barking and carrying on, unlike her usual quiet self. When I first got her I'd even asked the vet if there was something wrong with her voice box. She was that quiet. I peeked out the window and got another shiver.

Dusk, standing there with a six-pack in hand.

I thought about ignoring him, but I couldn't fake not being home. Mollie'd given us away.

"Mr. Bradshaw? Are you in there?"

No good ever came from being called Mr. Bradshaw, but I opened the door anyway. "Er ... hello, Dusk. What brings you round?" The beer was obvious, but the reason wasn't.

"I just thought we could chat a while and have a beer or two. Or more if you like." That strange laugh again.

He'd cleaned up nice, making an effort, and I reckoned the boy was lonely. Maybe not long outta prison. I got Mollie calmed down, opened the screen door, and stepped out onto the porch. For some reason I didn't want him in my house. I made excuses about the house being stuffy on such an unusually hot evening, but deep down I knew different. I ushered him toward the big maple tree between the house and barn.

We settled into the chairs I kept out there, and dang if he hadn't brought my favorite beer. He handed me one, popped the top on his, and started telling me about moving back to Laurel Falls. He'd been living in a hostel since he got out, not welcome to live with his daddy at the old family home. That word *family* made me shake my head, though I hadn't meant to.

Dusk picked up on it. "Yeah, some family, huh? My father doesn't claim me anymore. He's busy with his new family—and the new house he's building. Easier to start fresh than to deal with me and Astrid. Not that Astrid's done anything to be ashamed of. And of course, our mother is gone, though I barely remember her. That's partly why I came here."

"To Laurel Falls?" I asked, hoping that was what he meant.

"Well, yes, in part. But also to see you."

I felt a weight land on my shoulders like a rock-filled rucksack. I nodded and we sat like that for some time. My mind drifted back to the tumult of those days long ago. Neither Dusk nor Astrid had any idea their mother went off to live the high life in Washington, D.C. Their crazy father, Enoch, decided it would be easier on the kids to think of their mother as dead than to go through their lives knowing the truth.

Della, with a little help from me, found her and made certain she made payments to the father for the kids' well-being. I was wondering if that was still the case when I heard another pull-tab spew and Dusk say, "I was hoping you could tell me something about my mother. Did you ever meet her? And how did you find her body?"

Oh, how was I going to get round all those questions? Not truthfully, that was for sure. "It wasn't me who found her, Dusk. It was Della Kincaid." That was at least true, as far as it went.

"But Astrid said you helped."

"I did, yes." I turned toward the man, who at that moment looked so hopeful my heart ached. I told him all I could, explaining that I'd barely met her. Again, the truth if I stopped there. Besides, he didn't need to know all the dirty details about his mother.

When I'd finished, he sighed and swallowed the last of his beer, then crushed the can with one strong hand. I looked at my watch, hoping our evening was coming to a close, though I had to admit it'd been more enjoyable than I'd reckoned. Except for those prison tats, he seemed to have grown up okay. Then he threw me back on my heels.

"I asked around and heard you sometimes rent out your guestroom. I need a place to stay. That hostel is just one step up from ... well, you know."

I felt uneasy all over again. Was he checking up on me, what with bringing my favorite beer and knowing about my spare room? I'd allowed plenty of folks to live in the guestroom I'd fixed up out in the barn. Nigel Steadman; Duane Dockery; Shiloh, my woodworking partner, who'd moved in and outta there more times than I could count. Even an FBI agent. But an ex-con? *Well*, I thought, *at least I don't have to worry about the safety of the boys with an ex-con living on the farm, but what about* my *safety?*

Dusked noticed my unease and stayed quiet for a change. Even Mollie sensed it. She came over and licked my hand. I took that as a sign. I said, "First I need to know what sent you to prison."

After Dusk, along with all the other Appalachian Mountain Mysteries, is available at most online retailers.

Lynda McDaniel Books

FICTION

Waiting for You
A Life for a Life (permafree)
The Roads to Damascus
Welcome the Little Children
Murder Ballad Blues
Deep in the Forest
Up the Creek
Unwrapped
After Dusk
Deep South Trouble
Appalachian Mountain Mysteries Box Set
A Life for a Life Audiobook

NONFICTION

Words at Work (permafree)
How Not to Sound Stupid When You Write
How to Write Stories that Sell
Write Faster Series Box Set

www.ingramcontent.com/pod-product-compliance
Lightning Source LLC
Chambersburg PA
CBHW051155130726
47988CB00005B/2132